Lamort DeLioncourt

The
Palace Hotel
SHORT GAY ROMANCE

WARNING

This book contains sexually explicit scenes and adult language. It may be considered offensive to some readers. This book is for sale to adults ONLY.

* * * * * * * * * * * * * * * * * * *

Please store your files wisely where they cannot be accessed by underage readers.

Please feel free to send me an email. Just know that these emails are filtered by my publisher. Good news is always welcome.

Lamort DeLioncourt – **lamort_delioncourt@awesomeauthors.org**

About the Publisher
4Fun Publishing, a member of **BLVNP Incorporated**, 340 S. Lemon #6200, Walnut CA 91789, info@blvnp.com / legal@blvnp.com
NOTE: Due to the highly emotional reaction of some people to works of erotic fiction, any email sent to the above address that contains foul language or religious references is automatically deleted by our anti-spam software and will not be seen. All other communications are welcome.

DISCLAIMER
Please don't be stupid and kill yourself. This book is a work of FICTION.
Do not try any new sexual practice that you find in this book. It is fiction and not to be confused with reality. Neither the author nor the publisher or its associates assume any responsibility for any loss, injury, death or legal consequences resulting from acting on the contents in this book. Every character in this book is over 18 years of age. The author's opinions are not to be construed as the opinions of the publisher. The material in this book is for entertainment purposes ONLY. Enjoy.

The Palace Hotel

Short Gay Romance

By: Lamort DeLioncourt

© Lamort DeLioncourt 2014
ISBN: 978-1-62761-694-2

Chapter 1

The plane from Paris was running late as usual and I had been at the Marseille Airport far too long already. I was waiting impatiently for John to arrive so we could begin our annual holiday. Because his business kept him in the US for extended periods, we had not seen each other for almost six weeks. I needed the chance to touch, feel, and caress the man I loved.

I knew that the 24-hour total travel time would have him worn out, but he had gotten the best connections possible from Los Angeles. The idea of spending 16 hours sitting on an airplane made my blood run cold, but he did it without compliant a dozen times a year. Unfortunately, we still had the flight to Zurich to contend with, as we were going on holiday to St. Moritz. It was only a five-hour trip, but on top of everything else, it seemed almost cruel to do to him.

While drifting through my thoughts, I heard the speaker system announce the arrival of his flight from Paris. I waited impatiently for him to disembark. Once he was past the security area, I lunged at him, grabbing him and hugging him tightly. I whispered my love and joy at his arrival. He squeezed me in return before planting a wet kiss on my burning lips. He looked tired, but not completely destroyed by the trip. We still had a short delay before our flight to Zurich.

We made our way to the bar to await the departure of our flight to Zurich. Once we had our champagne, we sat at a small table in the corner and he told me of his business dealings and the grueling trip from Los Angeles.

I told him we could cancel our plans for St. Moritz and spend our vacation at home, here in Aix-en-Provence. He assured me that he wanted to go to St. Moritz, and was willing to suffer through another flight and a train trip to get there.

While we talked, I felt him slide closer to me, and soon his arm was around me and his thigh was rubbing against mine. He kissed me deeply, and then whispered in my ear how much he had missed me. His actions and words sent shivers down my spine, and lit my internal fires. Had we not been in a public place, I would have torn his clothes off and let him ravish me on the spot. I reached my hand to his pants, and felt the familiar firmness between his legs. I squeezed and massaged him, and as I did, we heard the speaker system announce the departure of our flight to Zurich. We grudgingly ended our embrace and headed to the departure gate.

After our arrival at the boarding gate, we boarded immediately. The flight attendant showed us to our seats and offered to help with the hand held luggage. The flight attendant immediately served us Champagne, to help pass the time until departure. While sipping the wine, we chatted about getting to St. Moritz and beginning our holiday.

With the wine glasses removed, we prepared for takeoff. Without further ado, we taxied to the tarmac and began the long roll down the runway. In no time, we were airborne, and the flight attendant returned with fresh wine glasses and a bottle of private stock Champagne. He opened the bottle for us and poured. He also told us that the flight was nearly empty and that we had the first class cabin to ourselves.

We put the armrest dividers up and made our seats into a small loveseat. John slid over to me, and put his arm around my shoulder. He then tickled my ear with his pinky finger, driving me crazy with desire. This was his signal to me that he needed to have his pénis serviced.

We rang for the attendant, and requested pillows and blankets. He adjusted the air conditioning jets, and brought us our pillows and blankets.

I gave the attendant a conspiratorial wink, wordlessly letting him know that we were about to engage in some mile-high fun. He responded by turning down the cabin lighting, and then assured us he would not disturb our privacy. He also told us to ring if there was anything we needed.

I wasted no time in getting our seats fully reclined, and the pillows placed for comfort. As John reclined and got comfortable, I let my hand drift down to his belt buckle and I released it. Then, gently grasping the zipper beneath it, I lowered it in a single pull.

Once the zipper was down, I opened the front of his pants as far as they would go, and started a slow, sensual massage of his pénis and scrotum through the silk of his boxers. As I felt his manhood stiffening, he lifted himself slightly to permit me to slide his pants and boxers down over his knees. Once fully exposed, I grasped his uncircumcised maleness and slowly retracted his foreskin. When fully retracted, I began a teasingly slow up and down stroking. After only a few minutes, he told me to stop teasing and get down to business, that he had not unloaded in two days, and needed to do so.

I quit the teasing and lowered my lips to his glans. I slowly took him into my mouth, sucking softly with my lips while running my tongue in circles around the head. I pulled his foreskin up over the head and let it slide over my tongue.

Once in place, I squeezed the foreskin closed with my fingers and allowed my tongue to swirl between it and the head, while I nibbled on his foreskin. John always liked this maneuver, and he responded with a soft moan and gentle upward push, forcing more of his stiffness into my mouth. I increased the amount of suction I was applying, and increased the stroke rate.

Soon I felt pre cum spreading outward from Johns' slit. His hands were soon on the back of my head and neck, and I knew he was ready to unleash his load. I increased the speed of the stroking, and licked his scrotum with each downward stroke. I felt the flesh-covered orbs pulling up close to his body and I knew he was almost there. Johns' breathing increased as my sucking increased.

Without warning, I felt his hands push me all the way down his cock, and I could feel him pulsing. With a quick scrape of my teeth up his shaft, I positioned myself to where I had only the head in my mouth. Using my tongue at lightning speed, I rubbed the sensitive underside, causing him to erupt. His semen poured into my mouth, allowing me only seconds between blasts.

I took a fast taste, and then swallowed, making room for the next shot. He pulsed eight times, before slowing to just a dribble. I managed to take all of his semen without losing a drop. I held the last of his semen in my mouth for a moment, savoring the flavor.

I finished swallowing, and sat myself up in the seat, while pulling the blanket over Johns' exposed groin. Just as I covered him, the attendant arrived with warm, lemon scented, damp towels so we could clean up. He also had more wine for us to enjoy.

Once I cleaned John, I pulled his pants and boxers up, zipped his zipper, and buckled his belt. He leaned against me, and was soon asleep, snoring softly in my ear.

The remainder of the flight was uneventful, and we arrived in Zurich nearly on time. As we prepared to disembark, the attendant was there to help with our carry-on luggage. As we left the plane, John slipped a $100 bill into the attendant's pocket, while thanking him for his attentiveness and discretion.

We made our way through customs to the baggage claim area. The Air France concierge provided luggage pickup, as well as an electric cart to take us to the train station under the main terminal of the airport. The ride was short on the cart, and we soon arrived at our train.

The train concierge met us on our arrival and arranged to transfer our luggage to the train. He then escorted us to our seats in the premier car. The car was beautifully appointed, and the seats luxurious. There was ample legroom, and a reasonable amount of privacy. He invited us to the club car for drinks, and informed us that the trip to Chur would be just over an hour, with a five-minute transfer to the St. Moritz train. The final leg of the journey was a three-hour trip.

After drinks in the club car, we returned to our seats and John reclined his seat back as far as it would go, and got comfortable. In minutes he was asleep, snoring softly. I smiled, leaned over and kissed him gently on the forehead. Then I turned to look out the window, and saw that a light snow had begun to fall.

Chapter 2

I continued to watch the snow falling through the train window. I must have fallen asleep, as the next thing I knew, the steward was gently waking us. We had arrived in St. Moritz. The steward informed us that our driver was retrieving our luggage, and we could disembark when we were ready.

As we exited the train, our driver had the car at the ramp for us. It was quite cold, but the snow was no longer falling. The driver held the door open, and we got into the car. The heater was running, and the interior of the car was toasty warm. We settled ourselves in as the driver closed the door. The driver introduced himself to us, telling us his name was Maurice, and told us he would be taking us to the hotel. The hotel had thoughtfully provided a bottle of Champagne, which he opened and poured for us. John and I toasted each other and the start of our holiday.

It was a short ride to the hotel. As we pulled up in front, the doorman met us, opening the car door, welcoming us back to Badrutt's Palace. Heinrich always provided a genuinely warm welcome to us. A bellhop appeared and began unloading the luggage. John provided the customary $50 gratuity to Maurice while thanking him for his service.

Heinrich escorted us to the impressive lobby doors, opening them gracefully for us. We stepped into the lobby, and the feeling of being home washed over us. John smiled at me.

We began making our way to the check-in counter, when Émile, the concierge, met us. He assured us that our check-in had already been taken care of, and pressed the room key into John's hand. He steered us across the lobby to the bar and offered us drinks, as our suite was not ready for occupancy, the femme de chambre still putting the final embellishments on it. He led us directly to our usual table by the large windows that overlooked the lake.

John told me about his latest business dealings while we sat. He also let me know how well the company was doing. I smiled as always, feigning interest in the business. John was my life and my interest, not the business. We had time for one glass of Champagne before Émile returned to our table and told us the room was ready whenever we wanted to go upstairs. We told him we were ready, and he escorted us to the elevator. Once we arrived on our floor, he took us to our room. While John fumbled for the key, Émile slipped his master key into the slot and opened the double mahogany doors for us.

The smell of fresh cut flowers wafted through the air as we entered. The floral arrangements were beautiful, and there was a large fresh fruit basket on the living room coffee table. Émile gave us the usual quick guided tour through the suite, and informed us that our luggage had been unpacked. Our tuxedos were at the laundry for wrinkle removal and our shoes were out for dressing and polishing. He made his way to the coffee table, and asked if we wanted him to open the Champagne for us. John told him no, we were not quite ready for Champagne. As he excused himself, he surveyed the room one last time, making sure everything was in place. I thanked him for all his thoughtfulness, and John extended his hand to him, pressing a $100 bill into his palm, also thanking him. As he exited the door, he informed us that our butler would be Jacques, and he would be arriving shortly to help us settle in. With that, he backed out of the room, closing the doors behind him.

Finally alone with John, I lunged at him, planting one of my most passionate kisses on his warm lips. John wrapped his strong arms around me, pulling me to him, while driving his hot tongue into my waiting mouth. He allowed his hands to slip down to my buttocks, where they began a soft, sensual massage on the tender skin. I felt myself hardening at his touch. I slipped one hand between us and allowed it to work its way down to John's groin. I had barely reached the top of the zipper when I felt his hardness strain against the material of his pants. I could tell from the throbbing that he was ready to lose his clothes, and get into some serious lovemaking.

I worked his belt buckle loose, and allowed his pants to slide to the floor. His erection was straining, struggling for release from his tight boxers. A small spot of wetness had already formed on the material. John took hold of my shirt and attempted to unclasp the buttons. He was not having any success, and in his frustration, he tore my shirt off, sending buttons flying. Wanting to keep my pants in one piece, I quickly unbuckled my belt and let my pants fall to the floor.

John leaned over, took my nipples in his fingers, and began a squeezing, twisting motion. I felt my spine start to tingle. I managed to slip down enough that I could get his nipples in my mouth. I licked and sucked each one individually, while he continued caressing mine. Soon I felt the familiar push of his hands on my shoulders, encouraging me to go lower. I slowly slid to my knees, which placed me directly in front of the bulge of his boxers. I could see his manhood straining against the fabric. My fingers made their way into the opening of the boxers and grasped the raging beast they found. With my free hand, I reached around to John's buttocks and slipped my fingers into the waistband of the boxers, pulling them gently down. As the boxers made their way to the floor, his erection sprang free, slapping against my lips, as if to demand immediate attention. I allowed myself the luxury of tasting the crown of his phallus, with the foreskin in place. With my tongue, I slid into it, the tip of my tongue finding the head of his tool already slick with juice. Intent on my task; I gently rolled back the foreskin, fully exposing the crown. I leaned in, took the entire head into my mouth, and gave it a tongue-lashing that would excite even a dead man. John began softly moaning as my tongue attacked the sensitive head. He soon had his hands on the back of my head, forcing more of his maleness into my mouth. I opened my mouth wider and allowed him to force as much in as he wanted. Not surprisingly, he soon had all of it in my mouth and I found myself deep throating him. He began the usual thrusting, and I continued to enjoy the slapping of his couilles on my chin. John increased his thrusting movements, and I knew he was on the verge of shooting. Juice was pouring out of him, and I could feel the pulsing of his head with each inward thrust. I applied maximum suction and began massaging his scrotum. The combined actions pushed him over the top, and he began shooting his load into my mouth. The first blasts were savage, striking the back of my mouth and racing down my throat. I barely had time to taste it before the next volley was flying across my tongue. After three or four shots, the semen slowed and started to dribble out of him. This allowed me the opportunity to taste his sweet juice. As I cleaned him up, he looked down smiling at me.

I sat on the floor, and scooted over to the sofa, leaning back against it. John joined me and we sat naked enjoying the afterglow of our heated encounter. John draped his arm around my shoulders, and pulled me to him.

After a few minutes, John got to his feet and helped me up. He went over to the wine bucket and pulled the cool Champagne from the ice. With practiced expertise, he slipped the foil off and loosened the cage. He took the towel wrapped bottle, and slowly turned it until the cork made the traditional "pop". He gently poured the wine into the flutes and handed me mine. We toasted each other and our love, slowly sipping the wine. We made our way to the sofa and sat down, the leather cool on our warm skin. We finished our first glass, and John poured us a second.

As he poured the wine, I took note of his nakedness, the outline of muscles showing under his skin. My eyes made their way to his face, and I found myself staring into his dark eyes. They held a look of exotic mystery that promised much more to come, before this holiday was over.

Chapter 3

Jacques had provided soft pillow fluff robes, and as we sat sipping our wine, John reached over and grabbed them. He slipped into his, and held mine up so I could slip into it.

John padded slowly over to the French doors, indicating I should follow him. He opened the doors and we walked out on to the balcony. The air was absolutely still, and the mist from our exhaled breaths hung frozen in the air. Though the temperature was well below freezing, I didn't immediately feel cold.

It had started snowing, and the view of the lake was stunning. The moon had fully risen, spreading its glow over the entire scene, reflected by the stillness of the lake. It was the ultimate in a perfect view. The romance the scene created was intense, making my heart swell as I gripped tightly on to John's arm. He pulled me closer to him, and as he exhaled, I could detect the aroma of the Champagne still on his breath.

We turned to go back inside, and John let his robe slip open, revealing his softened manliness. I could not help myself, and reached for it instinctively. He brushed my hand away and whispered, "*Pas maintenant Mon amour, mais bientôt*"- Not now my love, but soon. I was surprised that he had spoken in French, as he usually preferred English. I had to ask him, when soon would be. He gave me a wicked smile and winked.

My body always tingled when he spoke French to me. The softness of the words, and the emotion it conveyed was highly erotic.

Once inside, we picked up our wine glasses, and he refilled them. This emptied the bottle, and once poured, he returned the bottle to the bucket in a traditional upside down position. With his free hand, he took mine and steered us towards the bedroom.

Once inside, he turned and looked, gripping my waist and pulling me to him. "*Je t'aime,*" he said softly. I repeated the words of love, and we began a passionate kiss that could have set the room on fire.

When he broke the kiss, he asked if I would join him in the Jacuzzi tub. Wasting no time in responding, I nodded my head yes, and went over to start the water. Once again, Jacques had anticipated our needs, and left us yet another bottle of champagne on ice. I handed the towel and bottle to John, and he wasted no time cracking the seal and popping its cork. The cork hit the ceiling, and ricocheted into the tub.

=oOo=

John slipped his robe off, and stood near me in complete nakedness. I could feel the heat radiating from his body. I bent over the tub, and added rose scented bath salts to the water. John took this opportunity to push my robe aside, and slide his now hardening manhood between the cheeks of my buttocks. I loved the feel of him between my cheeks, not just for the feeling of intimacy, but also for the feeling of anticipation. As he slowly rubbed himself against me, I could feel my sphincter begin the rhythmic squeezing that signaled my willingness to accept John deeply into me. I expected him to penetrate me, and prepared myself.

Once again, I was to hear the words "*Pas maintenant Mon amour, mais bientôt.*"

My heart sank, as I was fully prepared to feel John insert himself into me. He chuckled and told me he had intended to tease me, that love would happen after the Jacuzzi. He told me he wanted time to relax; his initial need for sexual release had been satisfied.

I felt him pulling at the back of my robe, and I slipped my arms out of it. Both nude, we stepped into the Jacuzzi. The water was hot and steaming, the aroma of roses filling the air. As I lowered myself into the tub, I slipped past John's maleness and took a moment to lick the tip and plant a quick kiss on it.

As we sat, I took the sea sponge and began to wash John's neck and back. As I massaged him with the sponge, I allowed myself to slide forward until my phallus was rubbing up against his lower back. Once I had washed his back, I told him to turn to face me. I was able to wash his face and neck, then sliding down to his nipples; I gave special attention to them, as I knew this area to be very sensitive. I continued downward, gently scrubbing his belly and abdomen. I continued lower, until I had a firm grasp on his manhood and couilles. I massaged him with gentle loving strokes, and he began to harden once again, his hardness floating in the bubbles. I gently washed his buttocks as he rose up from the tub. When I finished washing and massaging his feet, he was ready to turn on the jets. As the jets began streaming into the tub, the bubbles billowed up, and the scent of roses once again filled the air.

John leaned back against the wall of the tub, and allowed the jets to do their work, softening his tightened muscles, and releasing all the tensions of the trip and hours on the cramped airliners.

In mere moments, the combination of three bottles of champagne, and a warm Jacuzzi, was working their magic on John. He slowly slipped farther into the tub, as he began falling asleep. I released the plug from the tub and allowed the water to begin emptying. I took hold of John and woke him gently, getting him to stand while I put his robe on him. I managed to get him out of the tub and into the bedroom. We swayed like drunks trying to get to the bed, where I was able to support him while pulling the covers back. Once the bedding was ready, I got him to slip out of his robe and lie on the bed. I rolled him to his side, and pulled the sheets and duvet up over him. Instantly, he was snoring softly, as his breathing deepened.

I pulled my robe around me, as a chill touched my body. The room seemed a little cold. I adjusted the thermostat to warm the room slightly. I made my way to the living room and over to the fireplace. I found myself sitting down on the bearskin rug, gazing into the bright and cheery flames, as they chased the chill from me.

I don't know how long I had been sitting there, with random thoughts running through my head, but when I heard a soft knock at the door, I quietly called out enter, and the door slowly opened.

Jacques, our soft-spoken butler, quietly let himself in. He carried a silver tray with two steaming cups of chocolat chaud, and a small assortment of pastries. He lowered his voice even more, once he realized John was sleeping. He placed the tray on the small table next to the rug. He looked toward the bedroom and smiled. I smiled back at him, telling him that American business couldn't put John down, but three bottles of French Champagne could. He smiled back at me, nodding his head. He turned to leave with a parting "*Bonne nuit, dormez bien* (Good night, sleep well)."

I turned back to the fireplace and resumed gazing at the flames. Thoughts of love and passion raced through my head. I sipped the chocolat chaud, and slowly nibbled on a pastry, as I thought how lucky I was, to be here with the man I loved.

Chapter 4

I don't know how long I had sat staring into the fire, but I turned my head when I heard the door opening. It made hardly a sound, and I was soon able to see that Jacques was once again coming in to check on us. He said that he wanted to make sure that I had not fallen asleep on the rug.

He had a small silver tray with a large brandy snifter on it. The decanter was quite lovely, and the label was Jenssen Arcana Hors d'Age Cognac. It was such a fine cognac for a man of such simple tastes as me. Jacques set the tray on the table, and poured the cognac for me. As he poured, I realised that the fire was burning low, not providing as much heat as before. When he handed me the snifter, his hand touched mine and he exclaimed "*Mon Dieu*, you're cold."

I had not realized that my robe had slipped down to my buttocks, and was completely open in the front, exposing all of me to the cold. He pulled my robe up around my shoulders and closed it in the front to cover me.

He stood by me while I sipped the intensely wonderful cognac. When I finished, he asked if I needed a refill and I told him no, it was bedtime for me. He took my glass and put it down on the silver tray. He then went over to set the fire for the night. He adjusted the damper and added whole log pieces to the fire. The bed of glowing embers quickly ignited the new wood. When he was satisfied that all was done correctly, he returned to me.

He extended his hand to me, helping me get up off the rug, explaining that I didn't need to be spending the night on the cold floor. With a gentle pull of the hand and a lift under the arm, he raised me up off the floor. Once again he pulled my robe closed around me, and led me to the bedroom.

=oOo=

At the bedside, he turned my side of the bed down, and helped me slip out of my robe. I slid into bed, feeling the luxury of the Rebus linens. I again found my simple tastes pampered with such luxury. Jacques covered me and set the duvet. He turned the small night light in the bathroom on, and asked if I needed anything else.

I told Jacques that he had met every need I had. I told him that he had done all that needed doing and more. Once more he bid me *bonne nuit, dormez bien*, and told me that he would be retiring for the evening also, but that Henri would be available to take care of any needs we had during the night. I thanked him for his kindness and turned over in bed to spoon with John. I heard the door latch click as Jacques quietly let himself out.

I pushed myself back against John, causing his maleness to slide against me. I reached back and placed it between my cheeks. John stirred a little as I adjusted him. I then reached back and pulled his arm over me so it draped across my chest. I again pushed back until my back was against his chest. I pulled the covers up over our shoulders. I settled myself, and got very comfortable.

Just as I was about to drift off to sleep, I felt John's hand squeeze my right nipple. I also realised that his soft, flaccid pénis was now firm and ready for use. He leaned against my ear, whispering that now was the later he promised earlier in the evening.

I smiled to myself, slipped my hand down between us, and gave his phallus a loving squeeze. In short order, he was fully erect and ready. I began the squeezing of my sphincter, signaling to him that I was ready for him to begin.

He wasted no time in retrieving the lubricant from the nightstand. In a flash, I felt his fingers, wet and slick, begin to probe me deeply with a slow massaging action. When his fingers touched my prostate, I went over the top with delight and demanded that he stop teasing, and get his hardness into me. He told me to be patient, that all would happen in time. He withdrew his fingers, and I could feel him lubricating the head and shaft of his tool. I could feel his hand guiding his erection towards me. It was only moments before he touched me. I immediately pulled my knees to my chest, and pushed back against him, causing his manhood to penetrate me. Without hesitation, he pushed his entire pole into me with a single stab, hitting my prostate and making me feel like I would ejaculate instantly. I was delirious with the intense pleasure racing through me.

I felt his lips and tongue licking my ear as he began his push and pull motion. With each forward thrust, I pushed back to achieve the deepest penetration possible. The head struck my prostate with each inward thrust, causing me to gasp with delight. His hand continued to play with my nipples, keeping them rock hard. He reached down between us, and retrieved some juice from my phallus. His lubricated fingers returned to my nipples and began a slick massage of them.

My own maleness fully hardened with his continued thrusting. I reached down to stroke it, while he continued the nipple play. I loved each deep inward thrust that he gave me. The repeated contact with my prostate was making me leak copious amounts of juice, which made my stroking much more slippery. I was thoroughly enjoying myself when I felt John once again lean into my ear. This time however, he whispered that he wanted to shoot in my mouth and not in my anus.

I quickly turned over and slid down his chest and abdomen. I took him in my mouth and began working on him. It was mere seconds before I heard him gasp and then thrust deeply into my throat. His seed exploded, racing across my tongue and down my throat. He blasted at least four times before he began to slow his thrusting, and his explosion became a dribble on my tongue. I made sure to clean him completely, before allowing him to withdraw. I so loved the taste of his seed. Once I was done cleaning him, I used my lips to pull his foreskin back up over his now sensitive head.

Once finished, he spooned up against me and reached over me to grasp my maleness. I told him he didn't have to, but he insisted. His hand began a slow and steady stroking action on me. As he stroked my circumcised pole, he again lamented the fact that there was no foreskin to play with. I reminded him that I had not been snipped by choice, and if I could grow it back, I would. He took the head between his finger and thumb, rubbing the juices all over. He then gripped the shaft and began to stroke me in earnest, sliding his juice slicked fingers from the base to the tip. My skin quickly dried out and he stopped long enough to spread lube all over the palm of his hand. He returned to the stroking, and I began to enjoy it more. Soon I was pulsing and thrusting against his hand. He knew I was about to go over the top, and stopped stroking and just squeezed me in his hand repeatedly. This was enough, and I began spraying all over his hand and the bed linens.

When I was finished expelling my fluids, he brought his hand up to my mouth and fed my seed to me. I loved the taste of my own seed almost as much as his.

We settled back down and got comfortable against each other, once the after play was finished. John spooned me from behind, wrapping his arms around me, and me pushing back against him. I felt him put his pole between my cheeks again, and heard him exhale with contentment. Soon his gentle snoring signaled that he was asleep.

I allowed myself to relax, and soon fell asleep, feeling very satisfied.

Chapter 5

I woke to the sound of the door opening and a service cart being brought into the room. Jacques rolled it to the bedroom and parked it. He then went to the windows and pulled back the drapery hiding the French doors. The sun was well up, and flooded the room with warm light. Some of the rays reached the bed, providing immediate warmth. Jacques made his way over to the fireplace and added wood to last night's embers. Soon a crackling fire was spreading heat through the room.

I reached over the other side of the bed and found that John had already slipped out. He was an early riser, and often let me sleep in. Jacques saw me reaching and let me know that John had been up at dawn. Apparently, he decided that he wanted to go skiing this morning. Since I did not ski, he left me sleeping. Jacques told me he had provided John with café and croissants in the lobby while he waited for the service car to take him to Corvatsch.

Jacques came over, straightened the duvet, and propped me up on pillows. He then reached around to the service cart and picked up the brass bed tray. He carefully positioned it and served me my usual café au lait. The coffee had a wonderful smell, filling the room with its aromatic essence. I could tell from the aroma that the café was from espresso beans. Jacques had put the sugar in for me before he added the milk.

As I lay sipping my café, I looked out the French doors and was able to see the far edge of the lake, and the mountains rising in the distance. A light dusting of fresh snow blanketed everything. There were few sights more beautiful than this view to wake up to.

I spent a few minutes contemplating yesterday's pleasures, and wondered what today would bring. John was fond of skiing in the mornings; the hotel provided him with special lift tickets that allowed him on the slopes an hour before the public. He would then come back to the hotel for lunch. While I contemplated the view and last night's passion, I thought there must be something I should be doing, but was unable to decide what, so I lay there sipping my coffee and appreciating the view.

While I was sipping my café and trying to plan the day, Jacques came to the bedside with my robe in his hands. He removed the bed tray, placing it back on the service cart. Next, he folded back the duvet and finally the sheets, exposing my nakedness to the cool room air. He helped me up from the bed and held my robe so I could slip into it.

Once in the robe, Jacques steered me to the bathroom, asking if I needed to relieve myself. I told him I did, and he positioned me at the toilet bowl. While I relieved myself, he started the shower running for me. Once he got me to the shower, he slipped my robe off and held the shower door open for me. I stepped in, and the warm water flooded over me, making my skin tingle. All the bathing necessities were on a small tray near the back of the shower, and Jacques asked if I would like him to wash my back for me. Since I never turn down an offer for such service, I told him of course. He took the sea sponge from the shelf, and coated it in perfumed soap. He then had me back up to the shower door so he could wash my back. His touch was firm but gentle on my skin. I felt the sponge moving down my back towards my buttocks.

Once he had the sponge low enough, he began scrubbing both my cheeks for me. He said nothing about John's sperm, which had become dried and crusty on me, and required additional scrubbing to remove. Once the sperm was gone, he washed the back of my legs and both feet. Once finished, he politely asked me to turn around if I wanted him to wash the front side of me. I gave it only a momentary thought, deciding that since this was a holiday, I should make the most of it. I turned around and presented my front side to him.

While I was turning to face him, he was rinsing the sponge and soaping it up again. Once I was fully turned, he applied the sponge to my neck and began working his way down the front of me. He again used a firm but gentle touch, which I found highly erotic. He lingered briefly at my nipples, using a circular motion of the sponge to wash them. His attention to my nipples caused my maleness to begin to harden. I did everything I could think of to try to distract myself and prevent a full erection from occurring. I was successful for a time, but once the sponge reached my navel and abdomen, I lost control and immediately hardened to maximum length. Jacques continued his downward washing, and soon had my tool in his hand, washing it. The feeling was delightful. Jacques paused his washing for a moment, and asked if he could ask a personal question.

I told him he was free to ask anything he wanted. He smiled and looked down at my pénis, and asked me what it was like not having a foreskin to cover the head. I explained that there was not much difference, except for masturbation, which now required much more lubrication since there was no foreskin to use for stroking. He then asked why I chose circumcision, andI told him that I had been born with a very tight foreskin, which I could barely retract.

On one occasion, John had pulled the foreskin all the way down, and I could not pull it back up. It was like having a tourniquet tightened around my pénis. I went to the hospital, where with a local anesthetic, they cut the skin, releasing the tightness and allowing the circulation to return. They explained that circumcision was the only permanent solution. I asked what would happen if I decided not to have it done, and they told me this situation would reoccur and I might find myself losing my pénis if the tight foreskin occluded the blood flow for too long. I decided at that instant that losing a foreskin was much better that losing a pénis.

While all this conversation was taking place, Jacques had tightened his grip on me and was now stroking me quite rapidly. He asked if I wanted to orgasm, and I panted out a yes. He continued his ministrations, and I found myself ejaculating all over his hand and the sponge.

Once I finished, he gently washed me off and had me step out of the shower so he could wrap a towel around me. He assisted me back to the bedroom, where I sat on the bed while he dried my hair and upper torso. He had me stand so he could finish drying my lower body. He took a second to pat my maleness and bollocks dry. Once I was fully dry, he helped me to get dressed. We moved into the living room, where he poured me a second cup of café and told me I had a 10:00 appointment to get my hair styled at the salon in the spa. With a smile, he turned and let himself out.

I sat sipping my café, thinking about what had just transpired, and decided that this was going to be one of the best holidays John and I had ever taken. I rarely had any type of sex with anyone unless John was there to watch. There was something exciting about watching him watching me and another man. On those rare occasions when John wasn't present, I always ended with a slightly wicked and naughty feeling. It was delightful.

The ringing of the telephone jolted me from my reverie. The salon was calling to remind me that my appointment was in 15 minutes. I quickly checked to make sure I was presentable and headed downstairs to have my hair styled.

When I arrived at the salon, Tristan, who told me he would be taking care of me during my stay in the salon, greeted me. He was a good-looking man, maybe 30 years-old, of medium build and fit body. His hair was dark brown.

He led me to his workstation and sat me down in his chair. He enquired how I wanted my hair styled, and I told him in any usual men's style he chose. He then helped me from the chair, and escorted me to the shampoo area. I sat in one of the laid-back chairs and enjoyed the scalp massage he gave me while washing my hair. He really did have magical fingers. I had to wonder how those fingers would feel on my genitalia. The mere thought of such a massage had me hardening in my pants.

As he helped me to an upright position, I tried to grab hold of the arm of the chair but ended up grabbing his groin instead. I immediately apologized, and he told me not to worry about it, that it happened all the time. The quick grab led me to believe that he was packing a larger than average pénis.

As I left the salon, Jacques appeared; he told me John wanted to have lunch in La Relais, one of the hotel's restaurants. He steered me to the lobby, and sat me at a small table next to the huge circular fireplace. Once seated, he indicated to a barman that my table required service. The barman nodded and headed for the bar. Jacques turned back to me and asked if I wanted to remain at this table or move to our restaurant table when it was ready. I thought for a minute before responding that since I could see the hotel lobby doors from this vantage point, I would wait here so I could see John when he arrived.

Moments later, the barman arrived at the table with a bottle of Champagne. Jacques opened and poured it for me. He asked if I needed anything else, and I told I did not. He turned from the table, and started towards the bar. He returned a few minutes later to inform me that John had just left the ski lodge and should be arriving in a little while.

As I looked out the lobby doors, I saw that a light snow had begun to fall and was already sticking to the road and buildings. I sat contemplating the possible after-lunch activities that John might be interested in, while I waited for him to arrive.

As I took the last swallow of Champagne from the flute, Jacques appeared to refill it for me.

I took the opportunity to thank him for the close personal attention he had provided to me in the shower. He smiled, and told me that Badrutt's expected the staff to meet all the needs a guest might have.

He also told me, that mine was the first circumcised phallus he had ever manually stimulated. He told me that European men were much more open to that kind of personal service, and his experience had been exclusively with uncircumcised pénises. He said he had seen many circumcised American and Middle Eastern men in the sauna and pool, and wondered what it would be like to provide that kind of service to them; however, they didn't usually have any interest in a man providing such a personal service.

By the time our conversation had ended, my flute was again empty, and Jacques again refilled it for me. Jacques moved back towards the front desk, and I returned my gaze to the lobby doors.

Chapter 6

While watching for John to arrive, I finished my third glass of Champagne. I decided to have another and reached for the bottle. Before I could get hold of it, the barman had come over, picked up the bottle, and poured my fourth glass. After he finished pouring, he enquired if I needed anything more. I told him no, and he made his way back to the bar.

I always enjoyed how attentive the staff at Badrutt's was to John and me. We had been coming here for years, ever since John's business had become a success. I never realized how lucrative the financial field could be. John had gained a reputation for insisting on excellent service, as well as being a very generous man when it came to gratuities.

As I looked up from my Champagne glass, I caught sight of the service car pulling up in front of the hotel. The doorman reacted swiftly, opening the door just as the car stopped. I saw John extricating himself from the vehicle.

At 6' 3" and 202lbs, John was a tall, imposing man. He had a large bone structure, and the muscles of a man who visited the gym several times a week. He visited the salon monthly to have his hair styled, and to get a manicure and pedicure. When working or entertaining clients, he always wore an Armani suit. His philosophy was that in order to be successful, one must look successful at all times.

I made my way to the entryway, and met John as he came through the doors. He spotted me, and gave me his best ear-to-ear smile. That smile made my insides melt. He stepped up to me and gave me a kiss on the cheek. He had changed into his apré ski clothes, which told me he had showered and changed clothes at the ski resort.

He asked if I was ready for lunch, and I told him, with a coy smile, I was ready for anything he wanted to do. He took my hand, and we walked over to the restaurant.

The maître d' greeted John by name as we approached him. He took us immediately to our table, which had a magnificent view of the lake. By the time he seated us, the waiter was arriving with our drinks. John was having his usual bourbon, and my bottle of Champagne from the lobby found its way to the table. Within minutes, asparagus crudités were on the table. John always enjoyed the fresh asparagus. When the waiter came to take our order, John decided on the duck confit with pommes de terre à la sarladaise. The potatoes were prepared with truffles and duck fat, and were one of John's favorites. I opted for the Salade Niçoise since I am always dieting. John finished his bourbon, and before he could put the glass down, the barman was delivering another.

We talked about how our mornings had been, John telling me how much he enjoyed his skiing adventure and how much I had enjoyed my morning shower. He told me he wished we could do this more often, but the business needed his constant attention. He then mentioned that he had met a German ski instructor named Gunther while at the ski resort. He told me that he was a very pleasant man, well built, and friendly. I told him I had always fancied German men and found them most interesting. John then asked if I thought I could manage a ménage a trios with him after lunch.

John's request did not surprise me, and I accommodated it. One of the ways that he found to exert his power over other men was to have sex with them. I long ago realised that it had nothing to do with love; it was more an animalistic alpha male behavior. It didn't matter whom John had sex with, he always came home to me. I was the one he said, "*Je t'aime*" to.

Lunch arrived, and while eating, I asked John a few questions about Gunther. John told me he was the quintessential Aryan boy. He described him as blonde-haired and blue-eyed nineteen year old. John told me he met him in the shower, and that he was uncircumcised with a phallus of about 6 inches. While finishing lunch, I told John that if he wanted to have Gunther join us, I had no objection. A little German dessert was always a good thing. John signed the cheque, and we headed up to our room.

On the way to the room, John called Gunther on his cell phone and invited him over. Apparently, Gunther was quite pleased and indicated he would be right over.

When we got to the room, I noticed that Jacques had the chambermaids replace yesterday's flowers with new, fresh ones. Housekeeping knew to change the sheets daily, as I did not want to find dried semen on them when I got into bed. The chambermaids had straightened out the room, and everything was once again clean and sparkling.

While we were discussing our afternoon activities, there was a knock at the door. John opened it, and invited Jacques into the room. He had brought new bottles of Champagne and a small portable bar so John could have bourbon on the rocks. John looked at Jacques and then at me, and asked if I had enjoyed my personalized shower this morning. I laughed and told him I should have known he had something to do with the hand job in the shower. He smiled back and told me that since he had left early for the slopes, he felt a need to ensure that I had appropriate sexual satisfaction first thing in the morning.

I told Jacques we were entertaining a guest for the afternoon, and could he please make sure we had a supply of German beer for our guest. Jacques told us he would return shortly with the beer.

While John changed out of his apré ski clothes, I began filling the Jacuzzi with hot water. Jacques had mentioned using the hot water would reduce the time it took the Jacuzzi to reach the correct temperature.

I looked up from the tub, and was able to look straight through to the bedroom. John was standing at the window, looking out while changing his clothes. He had already removed his pants and underwear, showing off his very lovely, moderately hairy butt. As he finished removing his sweater and shirt, I marveled at his physical beauty. When he turned around to face me, I was able to see that his manhood was already semi-erect. He went to the bed, and grabbed the robe that Jacques and laid out for him.

I started for the bedroom to change, but a knock at the door stopped me. I went to the door and opened it. Jacques had arrived with the beer, and a third robe for our guest to use. He got the beer put away in the refrigerator and took the robe to the bedroom. I followed him so I could change. I went to my closet to hang my clothes, and as I took them off, found Jacques had followed me. He immediately helped me remove my sweater and shirt, and then helped with my pants and underwear.

As he drew my underwear to the floor, my pénis sprang from its confinement. I was also semi-hard. Jacques hung up my clothes, and helped me into my robe. He gave my pénis a teasing squeeze before turning to leave the room. He told us that he had already reserved our table for dinner, and instructed the maître d' to set the table for three in the event our guest joined us.

Once Jacques left the room, I made my way next to John. He put his arm around me and directed me to the French doors. We went out on the balcony. As always, the view was stunning and created a romantically charged atmosphere.

John leaned down to kiss me, and when his lips touched mine, an electric jolt coursed through my body. My pénis went to full erection. I felt John's tongue sliding between my lips, seeking entry into my mouth. I relaxed my mouth and his tongue slipped deeply into me. He explored every inch before thrusting his tongue in and out of my mouth, as if it were his manhood.

I leaned against him, and could feel his hardness pushing against me. Without interrupting the kiss, I slipped my hand down and released the belts of our robes, allowing them to fall completely open.

As his robe opened, John immediately pressed his phallus against my abdomen. He was rock hard and fiery hot. I allowed my hand to grasp him, and push his foreskin entirely off the head. This simple action caused John to grunt and begin pushing even harder against me. As I played with his foreskin, he started leaking juices in copious amounts. I ran my fingers through it and then used it to lubricate the head of his manhood.

When John finally broke the kiss, he kissed my neck and then tongued my ear, driving me to near insanity. He then whispered he wanted me to service him orally. We turned and stepped inside.

As I began the slide to my knees, John grabbed the neck and shoulders of my robe, pulling it off me. When I finally reached his hardened pole, I was completely naked. For whatever reason, John felt that anyone servicing him orally should be naked.

I started my service with some gentle handwork on his shaft, which caused his foreskin to slide up and down. As I pulled upward with his foreskin, juices flowed like a river. Not wanting to waste any of John's fluids, I leaned in and began a thorough licking of the shaft and head. I scooped the juices up with my tongue and drew it into my mouth. Oh, how I loved his taste.

As I continued my work, there was a knock at the door. John didn't care who saw me fellating him, and he said come in. I turned slightly to see, and there was Gunther coming in the door. He was all that John had said.

John invited him to join us, telling him with a laugh, we had decided to start without him. Gunther came over to us, surveying the scene before him. There was John wearing a fully open robe, and me, naked on my knees, sucking him. I saw Gunther's pants start to tent as he stared at the erotic scene.

John withdrew from my mouth, turning to greet Gunther. John pulled him to us and began kissing his neck. I took advantage of the moment and released Gunther's belt, allowing his pants to drop to the floor. He was wearing a white jock strap instead of underwear. I reached to pull it down, but he gripped it to prevent its removal. I wasn't sure why he wanted to keep his jock on, but I left it alone and I stood up and unbuttoned his shirt, tossing it onto the bed.

John told me to service him, and I looked at Gunther, wondering about the jock strap. He said he did not want the jock strap off until he was fully hard, because he felt that his pénis was rather small when limp.

I slipped back down to my knees, and started rubbing my hand up and down the front of the jock strap. Gunther was already semi erect, and I knew that with just a little effort, he would be rock hard. As I licked and chewed his maleness through the jock strap, I felt him fully harden. I reached for the waistband and slipped my fingers into it without resistance. I slid it down, lifting it over the swollen head. In a moment, it was around his ankles and he was kicking it off.

I took a moment to assess his meat, and had to agree with John about the size. Even fully erect he measured no more than 6 inches. Not being a size queen, I can work with any man's equipment. What he lacked in size he made up in foreskin. His foreskin over hung the head by at least 2 inches. Fortunately for him, I am good at foreskin foreplay.

I grasped him, and started pulling the foreskin back, licking the tip as the foreskin retracted. Once I had it fully retracted, I worked the head with my tongue and lips. Gunther started leaking juices almost immediately, and my tongue was flooded in it. I stuck my tongue fully out, and began pulling the foreskin up and over the head and my tongue. When my tongue was completely covered, there was still more foreskin to pull.

I continued working my tongue around his head, while stroking the foreskin up and down. I even attempted to blow his foreskin up like a balloon, with interesting results. When I deep throated him, my lips pushed the entire foreskin to the base of his pénis. It made quite a roll around the base of the shaft.

Once deep throated, he began a serious pumping in and out of my mouth. When he withdrew all the way, the foreskin slid back up the shaft and covered the head. With each inward thrust, the foreskin moved all the way back down the shaft.

I allowed him to control the depth and speed of each penetration, and felt him speeding up. His pénis began to swell and pulse, and as if on cue, he began dumping his load into me. I was surprised that he had prematurely ejaculated. I had been hoping for a more satisfying first experience with him. I had to work at swallowing, to keep from losing any semen from between my lips.

He must have jetted at least seven or eight times before subsiding to a dribble. His semen was bright and tangy tasting, as only a young man's can be. He was more sweet than salty, with a texture like heavy whipping cream.

Once I finished swallowing, I retracted the foreskin fully and licked him completely clean. Once clean, he jerked his meat out of my mouth, causing it to slap me on the cheek.

I turned to service John again, but he decided it was time for a break. He helped me into my robe and gave Gunther his. Once we all had our robes on, John led us out onto the balcony. We sat down, and John opened the Champagne for us. I told Gunther the beer was in the refrigerator, that he could help himself.

While Gunther was getting his beer, John came over to me and kissed me passionately. He slipped his tongue into my mouth and got a taste of Gunther's sperm. He then returned to his chair.

Once Gunther came back, John said he wanted a short break, and that we would continue after dinner. I told John that I would be more than happy to provide him with a quick cum, since he had not gotten off during the show. He shook his head no, and told me he was saving his sperm until after dinner.

We finished our wine and beer and headed inside to change into dinner attire. John and Gunther were nearly the same size, so John let him use one of the extra tuxedos he always traveled with.

As we dressed, I could not help but wonder what John had in mind for after dinner.

Chapter 7

Once dressed, we walked to the elevator. Our suite was on the sixth floor and the restaurant was on the lobby level. When the elevator doors opened, Jacques greeted us and held the doors while we boarded.

At lobby level, Jacques escorted us to the restaurant and signaled the maître d' to seat us. Our table was set and ready, and as we sat down, the maître d' removed the small reserved sign from the table. He greeted us and introduced himself as Maurice. He told us that André would be providing service for us. Maurice looked to the bar, and a barman immediately came over carrying a bottle of Champagne in an ice bucket. He placed it next to me, and went immediately back to the bar, returning to the table quickly, and bringing bourbon on the rocks for John and an Ur-Bock for Gunther. He opened and poured the Champagne.

As we sipped our drinks, André approached the table with the sommelier, and enquired if he could take our order. John smiled and asked him what he would recommend for an appetizer. He responded that the terrine foie gras was always good. John nodded his acceptance, and turned to the sommelier requesting a suggestion for a wine pairing with the foie gras. The sommelier immediately responded with a suggestion of D'Yquem 1988. John again nodded his head in agreement. John then ordered the Chilean Sea Bass, I ordered the French hen with foie gras, and Gunther ordered the steak. Obviously, Gunther was a red meat man. Once we had ordered, both men left the table.

Gunther had not said a word the entire time we were at the table, and I asked him if everything was all right. He said that everything was fine; the hotel and restaurant had just overwhelmed him. I enquired why he felt that way, and he told us in a low voice that he did not realise that people actually lived this way, and that he had never worn a tuxedo in his life. John and I both chuckled as John assured him that people did live this way, and he was fitting in just fine.

We spent a few minutes listening to Gunther tell us about his home in Bavaria, and how he was working as a ski instructor for the season to get enough money together for his spring tuition at the University. He told us he was studying to be a biochemical engineer.

As we listened to him, André approached the table with the foie gras and a freshly baked baguette. He served us, and made room for the sommelier to deliver the wine. The wine was slightly chilled, and the sommelier offered to pour John the first glass for tasting. John shook his head no, and indicated he preferred that he taste for us, as he was the expert. After he had thoroughly inspected and tasted the wine, he pronounced it excellent. John then asked him to pour for us. While he poured the wine, André cleared all the other drinks from the table.

As we ate the foie gras and drank the sauterne, which though sweet, paired well with the foie gras, we talked about the ski season and how nice it had been so far. I asked Gunther if he was bisexual or homosexual, to which he replied he was strictly homosexual. He told us he preferred to top, but was not averse to bottoming on occasion. I assured him that I was a dedicated bottom and would be happy to service both of them. They both smiled at each other.

André arrived to clear the table, and the sommelier removed the wine and glasses. He asked John if he wanted wine with dinner, and John told him to pair a nice wine for each of our dinners. When André arrived with our food, the sommelier was right behind him with our dinner wines and glasses. He had paired a wonderful white for John and me. Gunther received a very full-bodied red for his steak. Dinner finished uneventfully, and with the table cleared, John signed the cheque and we headed upstairs.

John opened the door for us, and both men allowed me to enter first. I noticed that Jacques had the chambermaid in to straighten up the room while we were at dinner. There were no signs of our afternoon party. I did notice that there was a sliver cloche on the coffee table. When I lifted the cloche, I found vanilla and chocolate puff pastries under it, both being my favourites. I also noticed that Jacques had placed several small silver trays around the room with Avanti condoms on each of them.

I went into the bedroom to change, and the guys followed me. I saw several more of the condom trays placed around the bedroom. Our day clothes were in the closets, and there were three fleece robes on the closet door hangers. I got out of my tuxedo quickly and slipped into the robe. While John and Gunther finished changing, I went out to the living room and found Jacques setting the fireplace for the night. He had already put a tray with café and chocolat chaud next to the pastries. He asked if he could go into the bedroom and set the fireplace in there for the night. I told him to go right ahead.

The bedroom door was open, Jacques knocked, and as he walked in, he found both John and Gunther naked, putting on their robes. Gunther was semi-erect and displaying his long foreskin. Jacques smiled and headed directly to the fireplace to bank it for the night. Once done, he exited to the living room.

By this time, all of us were in the living room, and John mentioned to Jacques that he was welcome to join us for the evening. Jacques smiled and told us his wife might not be pleased with the idea. John responded with a, so who is going to tell her? Jacques took a moment to think, and then told us his shift would be over at midnight. With that comment, he turned and made his way out the door.

Once he was gone, John asked us to sit down. When we did, he explained that the evening was for everyone's pleasure and enjoyment. There was to be no pain inflicted on me and that Gunther was required to wear a condom if he planned to mount me. With that said, I stood up and dropped my robe to the floor. I went over to John and pulled his robe open, exposing his beautiful pénis. I immediately grabbed it, and pushed the foreskin down. Once the head was exposed, I took it in my mouth to give it a tongue bath. John spread his legs wider, so I could get to and massage his bollocks with my free hand.

While I began working on John, Gunther came over the sofa and

John invited him to join us. Once seated, he opened his robe, exposing his tool and the blonde bush surrounding it. He was completely hard, his pénis standing at a 45° angle to his body. Even though he was fully hard, his foreskin overhang was long. His bollocks had the same blonde hair that surrounded his tool. His skin was so white, that it appeared translucent.

I reached out to him, and took his manhood in my hand, pulling him closer to John. Once hip to hip with John, I began peeling back his foreskin. With the foreskin pulled completely back, I was able to see that the head was dark red in colour, and very moist. I started pumping his tool and then I returned my mouth to John's sausage. With each bob of my head on John's manhood, I pulled Gunther's foreskin tightly down, and then back up. In very little time, Gunther was softly moaning and grunting from the hand job he was receiving.

I felt John tap me on the shoulder, and when I looked up, he indicated that he wanted me to fellate Gunther. I let John slip from my mouth and pivoted towards Gunther. I grasped his bollocks with my free hand, and pulled his foreskin all the down with the other. I took him in my mouth, and put my tongue on the underside of the head. I pulled his foreskin all the way up, covering the head and my tongue too. I began circling the head and applying light suction to his organ. In mere moments, Gunther gave a sharp intake of breath, his maleness swelled to its maximum size, and the pulsing began. I knew his climax was eminent. All I could think of was oh no, not another premature ejaculation. He drove himself into me as deeply as he could, and then started shooting his load, and as he did, I applied a moderate pressure to his bollocks. I increased the suction, deep throated him, and allowed him to pump his entire load directly down my throat.

Once he was finished, I began backing off him. When I had only the head in my mouth, I gently nibbled on his long foreskin, which caused his manhood to begin to harden. I did not want round two with him just yetthough, so I cleaned him up and let him slip from my mouth, while pulling his foreskin up.

I returned to John, set on getting his load in my mouth. While I fellated him, John, not being a shy man, asked Gunther if he always prematurely ejaculated. Gunther, looking embarrassed, blushed and shook his head no. He told John that he had never had his peter sucked quite like that before. He then told us that the feelings were so intense, he lost all control of his body. John smiled and told him he understood.

I continued my bobbing motion on John's meat, increasing the suction and speed, while I massaged his bollocks. He told me he wanted his bollocks licked and sucked, and I complied immediately. John's bollocks were quite large, and I had to work at taking them both into my mouth at the same time. While I licked and sucked, John began leaking precum copiously. I licked his shaft to the top and used my tongue to get all of it on my tongue. Oh how I loved the taste of John's juice. John took hold of my ears, indicating he was ready to climax, so I deep throated him repeatedly until he fired off his load. When done, I cleaned him up, and let his softening member slip from my lips, while pulling his foreskin back into place.

I got up off the floor, sliding my robe back up over my shoulders. John looked questioningly at me, and I told him I was not yet ready for round two. I explained that I wanted some Champagne before we continued the adventure. The only bottle in the room was very warm, so John called down to have Jacques bring up a new one. I sat down on the sofa between them.

We talked while we waited, and Gunther finally got up the courage to ask me if he could have me anally. I told him to ask John, as I was his, and would do anything he wanted. With a slight smile, John looked at him and nodded affirmatively.

Chapter 8

John smiled at me, and turned to answer Gunther's question. He told him that he had no issue with him enjoying me anally, but that I would have to agree to it, and he reminded him he would have to wear a condom.

I looked over at Gunther and gave him my coyest smile and nodded my head yes. I didn't have any concerns about him mounting me, as he was smaller than John was in both length and girth. I knew I could easily accommodate him. I saw him looking around the room, and he smiled when he located the condoms Jacques had placed for us.

By this time, Jacques was knocking at the door with our Champagne delivery. Since I was the only one with a robe on, I answered the door. As expected, Jacques was at the door with this silver service cart. The Champagne was sitting on ice in a sliver wine cooler, and the flutes were upside down on the service tray, on white linen napkins. I invited him in, and moved out of the way so he could get the service cart in.

As he entered, I noticed his eyes making a quick scan around the room. His gaze stopped at the sofa where John and Gunther were sitting naked. He rolled the service cart to the table, and opened and poured the Champagne.

John invited him to take a moment and have a glass with us. He told us he would like to, but hotel rules didn't allow the staff to drink with the guests if they were on duty, and his shift didn't end until midnight. I looked at the clock over the mantle, and saw that he only had 30 minutes left of his shift. I asked him if he could return in a half hour to join us in a drink. He smiled and said he would. As Jacques let himself out, the three of us returned to our conversation.

John asked if I was ready to continue the party, and I asked him if we could wait for Jacques to return. He replied that he was willing to wait. John and Gunther both got up from the sofa and slipped on their robes.

John headed to the French doors and stepped out to the balcony. Gunther was right behind him, with me bringing up the rear. There was no breeze, and the snow was light and drifting down slowly. It felt like the temperature was near freezing. I felt my pénis and bollocks shrink instantly, my body pulling them close to me for warmth. I looked at the other two, their genitals pulled up tightly against them. We stayed on the balcony long enough to take a couple sips of the wine, and then fled inside towards the fireplace. John asked if I was in a hurry to get back in and I told him I didn't need my manhood to get any smaller than it already was. John laughed, and told me he liked my little pénis, and I should be proud of it. I made my way to the fireplace and sat down on the rug, trying to draw heat from the fire to warm my very cold body.

John came over and sat down next to me on the rug. Gunther did the same on the other side of me. John snaked his hand into my robe, and grasped my tool. He told Gunther that he would have me fully erect in a few moments, and that then Gunther could decide for himself whether I was small in the equipment area. I shivered when he touched me, his hand cold to the touch, but I still felt the beginning of an erection. He opened my robe so he could get a better hold on me. With a dozen strokes, I was fully hard. John removed his hand and told Gunther to look. There was no embarrassment, as I was used to John doing this. Gunther leaned forward a little bit to get a better look. Before either of them could say anything, I told them both that, yes, I was small at only 5 inches, but I was very talented. I reminded them that I would look bigger if I still had my foreskin. They looked at each other, rolled their eyes and smiled. I also reminded them that since I was strictly a bottom, I only needed a talented anus and mouth.

=oOo=

Moments later, there was a knock on the door, and I went over to let Jacques in. He had changed out of his formal suit and tie. He was dressed in typical resort après ski wear. I opened the door fully and invited him in.

John and Gunther got up off the floor and sat on the sofa.

John poured Champagne for all of us. Jacques and I sat on the settee. After two flutes of wine, we were all feeling good. I saw Gunther's hand make its way to John's thigh, where he flipped back the robe, exposing John. He then began playful stroking of John. Jacques allowed his hand to roam to my upper thigh, and squeezed several times, before he opened my robe. I asked Jacques if he wanted to go to the bedroom and change, that there was still a robe on the closet hook. He said he did and headed for the bedroom. While he changed, I watched Gunther play with John. By the time Jacques returned in his robe, John was already fully erect.

Jacques sat back down next to me, and I wasted no time in opening his robe so I could see his pénis for the first time. He was of moderate size, larger than Gunther and I, but smaller than John was and he was uncircumcised. However, his foreskin only covered half of his glans. I took him in my hand and began the traditional up and down stroking, telling him I owed him one from this morning's shower play. He leaned back and made himself comfortable.

I decided to repay the mornings hand job with some of my renowned mouth work. I pulled his foreskin up as far as it would go, and wiggled my tongue under it. I made circular motions with my mouth, teasing the entire head. At several spots, the feelings must have been quite intense for him, as he grabbed my ears and moaned loudly. I continued working him, and suddenly he pushed me off his pénis, breathing quickly. He told me he was just about to unload, and he really didn't want to so soon.

I left Jacques's rigid, pulsing manhood and moved to John. I removed Gunther's hand from John, and replaced it with my mouth. He was extremely hard, and already pulsing. I retracted his foreskin all the way, and swallowed him down. He grabbed the back of my head, and forcefully pulled me farther down his shaft. He didn't stop pushing until his pubic hair covered my nose. I used my throat muscles to massage his hardness, while licking the lower half of his shaft with my tongue. He allowed me to please him for a short while, before indicating he wanted to mount me. I immediately released him, and asked where he wanted me.

John directed me to climb up on the table and spread my legs for him. As I took up the position, I felt John smack my buttocks playfully. He stood behind me, told me to reach back and spread my cheeks, and began rubbing his juice-slicked pénis up and down my cleft. He quickly found my anus and swirled the head around the opening. He used his shaft to force his juice into me, and then with one single thrust, mounted me. I moaned with intense pleasure as his bollocks slapped against me, indicating he was completely inside me. He held still for a moment so I could feel the pulsing of his rod, and then began slowly pulling out. He pulled completely out and repeated his single thrust push into me. I felt him stretching and pulsing, and he quickly started jackrabbit thrusting. He was obviously ready to shoot his load. I squeezed my sphincter as hard as I could, and I heard him moan and bury himself in me. A moment later, I felt his semen flooding into me with great force.

When he was finished, he lay over me, putting his chest on my back. After a brief pause, he licked my ear and nibbled on it. He whispered that he wished he had lasted longer, but my mouth work had been unusually sensual. As he slowly softened, he slid out of me. I could feel his semen dripping out of me. I felt him stand up, but I remained in my position. I didn't want all of his semen to run out. I squeezed my sphincter tightly. I wanted to save some, so that when Gunther mounted me he would feel the heat of my lover's semen in me.

I looked over at Gunther, and saw his wide smile and throbbing manliness. He was obviously pleased that his turn had arrived. As Gunther made his way over to me, I indicated to Jacques to come sit in front of me so I could take care of his throbbing tool.

Gunther was first to reach me, slipping up behind me and imitating John by slapping my buttocks. He took a moment to take the condom that John was offering, which he immediately put on without assistance. I was disappointed, as I enjoy putting condoms on my partner using my mouth. Pushing the base of the condom down the shaft with my tongue and lips is very stimulating for me. I spread my legs as far as I could, and he wasted no time finding my anus and roughly pushing himself into me. He was extremely inexperienced in pleasing a man, his lack of finesse showing. I obviously expected more from the boy. I hoped his earlier unloading would prevent a repeat premature ejaculation.

While Gunther began his thrusting into me, Jacques got comfortable and spread his legs, inviting me to pay attention to his hard manhood. I skinned his foreskin back, and began my finest lip and tongue work on his exposed head. I circled him with my tongue, while kissing and sucking on the head. He was already leaking juice, and I wasted no time licking it up. As I worked on Jacques, I realised that Gunther had already begun his rapid fire thrusting, indicating he was about to shoot his load. I squeezed my sphincter rhythmically, attempting to trigger his orgasm as quickly as possible, just to get it done. I knew I would get no satisfaction from him, so I just wanted him to finish. Sure enough, within seconds, he slammed himself deeply into me and I could tell even through the condom, that he was unloading. He grunted and groaned several times, before pulling his still rigid pénis from me with a popping sound.

I was disappointed that there would be no after play while he softened, but I was not surprised. He went back to the sofa and sat down next to John. After a moment, he reached down and pulled off the condom, throwing it into the fire.

Chapter 9

I could tell from the look on John's face, that he knew I was disappointed in Gunther's lack of skill in lovemaking. I didn't have a problem with inexperienced young men; I just expected to have the opportunity to teach them how to love a man. I had hoped that Gunther would ask about ways to avoid his premature ejaculations, and provide satisfaction to the man he had mounted. Gunther was completely selfish, and obviously not interested in learning anything. He would have gotten the same satisfaction from a masturbatory toy.

I returned my full attention to Jacques, who I had managed to continue stimulating, while Gunther pleasured himself at my expense. He was quite stiff, and with each thrust into my throat, I could feel him swelling and pulsing. I assumed he would soon finish, and I would be left completely unsatisfied. He stopped thrusting; just allowing his maleness to sit on my tongue, while he explained that he didn't want to shoot too soon. He leaned close to my face, and unexpectedly kissed me on the cheek. When he broke the kiss, he whispered to me, "May I take you anally?"

I looked to John, who nodded his head. I looked back at Jacques and told him, "Of course."

Jacques' smile widened noticeably, and I felt his pole pulse on my tongue. While he slowly withdrew from my mouth, I tickled the underneath side of the head.

Before getting up from the sofa, he took the condom John offered, and asked me if I wanted to put it on him. I felt like he had read my mind. He was obviously well versed in male lovemaking, and knew the subtleties of pleasing a man. Instead of answering, I took the foil package from his hand and opened it. I slipped it a short distance over my tongue, before leaning over to his stiffness, and began sliding it down his shaft using my teeth to force the base ring down, while using my tongue to stimulate the parts already covered by it.

I took my time applying the condom to him, enjoying myself immensely. Judging from the grunts coming from him, he was also enjoying the condom application. Jacques was quivering from my ministrations. He was finding out how good it felt to have a condom put on. When I finally had the condom in place, I told Jacques I was ready for him to mount me. He stood up and made his way to my backside.

Unlike the first two riders, Jacques didn't slap my buttocks, instead he erotically massaged them with a light touch designed to inflame my already hot passions. He explored my entrance with his fingers. He was making sure I still had enough lubricant in me to allow him penetration without pain. John had left plenty of semen in me, to keep me well lubricated.

Once he was satisfied that I was ready, he stepped up behind me and rubbed his condom-covered pénis up and down my cleft. He made sure to rub at my manhole with every pass. He had my sphincter squeezing rapidly, as if attempting to grab him and pull him in. When I could not stand the stimulation any further, I begged him to mount me. He asked if I was sure I was ready, and I nearly yelled at him to stop teasing me and get inside me. John sat laughing at my plight. Jacques slowly slipped the head into me, and stopped. He teased me by asking if I wanted more of what he had to offer. I was nearly incoherent as I begged him to penetrate me all the way. He laughed, as did John, and began pushing his hardness into me a mere centimeter at a time. When I attempted to push back, he would take half a step back, preventing me from forcing more of him into me. He was in complete control of the penetration. I was helpless; he was in total control.

John continued laughing as Jacques unmercifully teased me. Jacques had reduced me to a quivering mass begging for the satisfaction I had so far been denied. Finally, he took pity on me and forced all of himself into me in a single thrust. My sphincter clamped down on him very tightly, and I felt every inch as he forced his way into me.

After completely filling me, He started to slowly pull out and push back in. He took the time to locate my prostate, and made sure he hit it with every thrust. By this time, my tool had been rigid and teased for so long, that I lost control and ejaculated all over the table. Jacques continued to thrust while I emptied myself, my sphincter squeezing him all the while. As I recovered, he leaned over me and asked, "Should I shoot now?" I told him if he was ready, so was I.

He lasted another minute or so, and then he groaned as he buried himself all the way into me. I felt his manhood swell and pulse before he stopped all thrusting and began to shoot his load into his condom. I could feel the heat of his seed through it. He shot a copious amount of semen into the condom, firing at least half a dozen shots.

Once finished, he remained in me until he began to soften. He pulled himself out and made his way to my head so we could see each other. He smiled at me, leaned forward, gave me a light kiss on the cheek and told me, "Thank you, for a beautiful ride."

As he reached to remove the condom, I stopped him. I slowly slid the device from his pénis, and cleaned the semen from him. Once done, I took the open end of the condom, placed it in my mouth and tilted it up, allowing his semento flow into my mouth. When I was done, Jacques returned to the settee smiling. I got up and sat beside him. I deposited the condom in the small waste can next to the settee.

John told us that he was very pleased with the show we had provided, that he had completely regained his hardness, and had once again begun pumping his juices in copious amounts. While he was making his comments, Jacques had retrieved the Champagne and wine flutes. He poured us all a glass of the wine and went into the bedroom to change into his clothes. Gunther refused the wine, and got himself another beer from the refrigerator. When Jacques emerged from the bedroom, he thanked all of us for a wonderful time, and explained that he had to get some sleep as he was working the next day.

Gunther realised the lateness of the hour and excused himself. He had early morning ski classes to teach. He quickly dressed and made his way to the door.

Once they had left, John pulled the settee to the French doors, and sat down inviting me to join him. He covered us both with the fluffy robes, and we sat watching the snow falling as we sipped our wine.

After a few minutes, John kissed me and thanked me for providing our guests a most pleasant time. He also apologized for Gunther's poor manners and performance. He told me he would not have invited him if he had realised he was a premature ejaculator without finesse. I reminded him that one never knows what one will get when picking up men in the showers. Then I laughed and told him that Jacques had more than made up for Gunther.

As we watched to snow falling with increasing intensity, I asked John if he was ready for bed. He said he was, but wanted to take a hot shower first. He invited me to join him. I made it a point never to refuse any invitation or request that John made of me, so I got up from the settee, downed my wine and headed for the bathroom to start the shower. Once the water was warm, I opened the door for John, and as he stepped in his hard pole slapped in on my leg.

I looked at him, and asked if he needed another round before bed. He thought about it for a minute, before answering yes. I asked him what he wanted, and he told me he wanted me anally. I offered oral stimulation to get him ready, and he told me it wasn't necessary. I asked him what was making him feel so sexy, and he told me that seeing Jacques kiss me twice had inflamed his passion. He said he needed to mark his territory again so any man approaching me would know that I was his. Though the words were rough, the sentiment was pure love. He made me feel extraordinarily special at that moment.

I moved to the front of the shower, and braced my hands on the support bar. I spread my legs and before I knew it, John was between them, forcing his manhood into me. He drove himself deeply into me, before drawing all the way back until he pulled out of me. He then plunged himself in again and went as far as he could. He struck my prostate, and my own hardness returned. He continued his rough ride, until my prostate was so over stimulated that I shot semen all over the shower walls and floor. With my sphincter clamping on him, John also began to shoot his load deep in me. Instead of stopping and unloading, he continued the pounding while he came. Once he was done, he laid his chest on my back, and nibbled on my ear.

"Don't ever forget that you are mine," he whispered.

We remained in that position for a short time, the hot water streaming over us. John finally withdrew, and we got out of the shower.

I toweled John off and sent him to bed. I dried myself and followed him.

As I slipped under the duvet, I could feel the heat from John's body warming the bed. I leaned over to give him a good night kiss, only to discover that he was already asleep. I kissed him lightly on the forehead, snuggled up to his side, and lay my head on his chest. He instinctively wrapped his arm around me, and pulled me tightly to him.

As I lay there drifting into sleep, I took a moment to give thanks for such a wonderful man.

Chapter 10

When I first opened my eyes, I could see the sunlight peeking through the opening in the drapes that covered the French doors. I figured it must be early, as I could feel John pushing up against my back. He normally left for the ski slopes just after sunrise. I also noticed that there was no scent of coffee in the air. I finally gave up guessing and looked at the clock on the nightstand. It was only half past five. I wondered why I was up so early, considering the late night we had.

My bladder was in need of emptying, probably due to the amount of Champagne I had consumed the night before. I slipped out of bed without waking John, and into my fluffy robe to ward off the early morning chill.

I made my way to the bathroom, and forced my hardened pénis to point downward towards the toilet. Once situated, my pénis softened, and my bladder began to empty.

I thought I would make my way to the living room, and take some heat from the fire. As I walked into the living area, I noticed that the settee that we had left in front of the French doors was back to its normal position. I also noted that the living area was once again looking fresh, there were no used condom wrappers in sight, and the flowers on the table were fresh. It is good to have a hotel staff that can anticipate ones needs.

I went over to the rug in front of the fire and sat down. My robe fell open, and the warmth of the fire rushed to my skin. It felt good to have the chill banished from me. I noticed that the fire was burning quite brightly, no longer banked for the night. I concluded that the night valet had been in earlier to stoke the fire back to life.

I sat comfortably on the rug, contemplating last night's

encounter. I still felt that Günther was a terrible disappointment. Unfortunately, I could not find any redeeming value in two episodes of premature ejaculation, and total lack of sexual finesse. Jacques, on the other hand, had turned out to be a welcome addition to an evening of sexual games. His manners and his finesse in lovemaking endeared him to my heart. I thought about the possibility of a repeat with him, and a smile spread across my face. I decided I would talk to John about it later in the day.

As I sat absorbing the heat from the fire, I heard a soft knock at the door. I thought it might be Jacques with café au lait. I said nothing and heard the passkey in the electric lock. As the door opened, a service cart entered first, followed by Henri. He pushed the cart towards the table. He was transferring the silver service tray to the table before he realised I was sitting in front of the fire.

He immediately offered, in his quietest voice, a sincere Bonjour, to which I smiled and replied in kind. He asked if I wanted café au lait, or would I like a cup of tea. I told him the café would be wonderful, and he began to prepare it for me. He inquired if John was awake yet, and should he prepare him café. I told him that we had been up quite late, and that John was still sleeping. He mentioned to me that Jacques had called in requesting to start his shift several hours later than scheduled, also pleading a very late night. The grin on his face made me wonder if he knew about last night.

He offered me a small tray with several pastries on it. I shook my head no, letting him know that the hour was far too early for me to eat. He asked if John and I wanted a European or English breakfast menu left.

I told him I normally ate a European breakfast, but John required the massive English breakfast to start his day. He left both menus on the table, asking that I call room service when ready to order.

As he prepared to leave, he asked if I would like assistance getting from the floor to the settee to drink my café. I raised my hand, and Henri took hold of it as well as my arm. He pulled me to a standing position and my robe opened completely. He gave a quick glance to my genitals before drawing my robe closed around me. He then helped me to the settee. Once seated, he asked me if I needed anything else before he left. I told him I was fine, and thanked him for his close attention to my comfort. He smiled at me, and excused himself. Jacques had told us that Henri was straight and never participated in man sex games. I thought that was a shame, as he was a very good-looking man and I would have liked to see him naked. I never heard the door close as he left.

As I sat sipping my café, I heard John in the bathroom. I went to check on him, wanting to know if he was really awake and ready for the day, or just up to relieve his bladder.

As I walked into the bedroom, John was exiting the bathroom. He looked up and smiled at me. I looked at him and could see that his semi-rigid manhood was jutting from the front of his robe. He came over to me, kissed me softly on the cheek, and whispered Je t'amie in my ear. I returned the kiss with a whispered Je t'aime. I then nibbled on his ear and kissed his throat.

I felt him harden, responding to the kissing of his neck. I asked if he required assistance with his hardness, or did he want to order breakfast. He told me that I was breakfast. With that, he guided me to the bed, sat me down, and stood with his maleness pointing directly at my mouth.

I wasted no time in moving in on him, starting by retracting his foreskin. Once peeled back, I took the tip into my mouth and swirled my tongue around it, cleaning the last drop of urine from him. I pulled off him for a moment, asking if he wanted to climax in my mouth, or did he want to bury himself in my backside. With a grunt, he slapped my cheek with his tool and told me to open my mouth. Judging from the roughness, I knew he wanted to quickly blow his load and get on with the day. These morning quickies were a common morning activity for John. He just needed to unload his semen so his lower head would allow his upper head to function through the day.

With minimal work on my part, John quickly buried his meat all the way down my throat, and began thrusting. I could tell from the urgency of the thrusting that his orgasm was not far off. I squeezed my throat muscles as much as possible, and he began to groan in pleasure. On his next pull outward, he shot his first squirt, jetting it across my tongue and down my throat. He then buried himself as far into my throat as he could, and finished unloading. While he was unloading, I massaged his bollocks to intensify his pleasure. Once done, he pulled out of my mouth and allowed me to clean the semen from his tool. When I was done, I looked up at him sweetly and asked if he was ready for café. He laughed and slapped his tool across my cheek one final time.

He helped me up from the bed, and held my hand as we walked into the living area for our café. We sat on the settee, and I served him his café

As we sat drinking the café, I felt his hand open my robe and squeeze my thigh, pausing for a moment before he took my soft pénis in his hand.

I pushed his hand away, and reminded him that he needed to get out to the slopes before the crowds became unbearable. He told me the slopes could wait, that my needs were also important to him. I laughed and reminded him that we could have sex anytime, but the slopes were only useable for a few hours in the morning.

He went to the bedroom, and when he returned, he was wearing his ski clothes and boots. He smiled as he headed to the door, a wide smile on his face. As he exited the room, I reminded him to leave the premature ejaculators at the gym shower. I heard him laugh as the door closed.

Once John was out the door, I sat down on the settee and poured myself a second cup of café. After drinking half of it, I made my way to the bathroom for a shower. In the bedroom, I found that John had not put on all of his layered ski clothing. I knew I should have dressed him. Now he would be cold on the slopes and not enjoy his time skiing.

I set the shower temperature control to 101°F. The water quickly warmed, and I slipped out of my robe, dropping it to the floor. As I stepped into the marble shower stall, I could feel the coldness on my feet. I stood under the delicate spray, and allowed the warm water to cascade over me.

I washed my hair and myself quickly, deciding to spend a little time in the Jacuzzi tub. I turned off the shower and went over to the tub to fill it. While the water was running, I went out to the living room to pick up my café. As I reached the table, there was a soft knock on the door. Since I was wearing nothing, I decided against answering it. If it were important, the person knocking would use their passkey. Only a couple of staff members could let themselves into the suite, so I wasn't concerned what they might see. Moments later, I heard the passkey in the lock and the door slowly opened.

Henri stepped in, and as he did, he looked over at me, and immediately apologized for the intrusion. I told him not to worry, that I had very little modesty.

He asked if he could come in and change out the towels. I told him of course. He made his way to the bathroom, and I heard him turn off the water in the Jacuzzi tub. As he tossed the old towels and robes out the bathroom door, he stuck his head out and told me the tub was ready for use.

I went to the side of the tub, and Henri offered me his hand to assist in getting into the tub. I took hold of him, and gently let myself down into the warm water. Once in the tub, he turned on the switches to activate the jets. Once everything was running smoothly, he turned to finish picking up the towels and robes from the floor. He went back out to the living room and I heard him at the door talking to the chambermaids in the hall. He quickly returned to the bathroom with fresh towels and robes. When he had them put away, he set out a towel and robe for me on the dressing chair. With that, he asked if I needed anything further. I told him no, and thanked him for his service. He then asked me what time would be good for the chambermaids to come in, change the linens, and refresh the room. I told him I would be going downstairs for breakfast as soon as I finished my bath. He smiled, nodded and walked into the living room. I heard him open the door and let himself out.

I think I was just a little bit disappointed that I had not had an encounter with Henri as I had had with Jacques the previous morning. My pénis had hardened and was insisting it needed attention. I squeezed my nipples for a few moments and then let my hands make their way down to my groin. With one hand, I began to stroke my tool, and with the other, I massaged my bollocks. I lay there with the jets massaging me, stroking my tool, and my mind fantasizing about last night. I quickly brought myself to orgasm, watching my semen swirling in the warm water as it exited my body. I watched as it floated around on the currents of the pool.

Once my orgasm had finished, I got myself out of the tub. I wrapped myself in one of the clean towels, and went into the bedroom. I dressed in my après ski clothing, put on my shoes, and headed downstairs for breakfast.

Chapter 11

In the restaurant, the host immediately seated me at our usual table, by the large windows overlooking the lake. My server arrived tableside pushing a serving cart. He enquired as to my preference for tea or café. I asked if he had English breakfast tea on the cart, and he nodded yes. He immediately setup the cup and saucer for me, and then added the tea bag and hot water for me after rinsing the cup with hot water to warm it. He asked if I required a French or English menu. I told him I didn't need a menu, that I wanted a large glass of orange juice, croissants with Camembert cheese, and crêpes with blueberries. He acknowledged my order and left the table.

My orange juice, croissants and Camembert appeared almost instantly. I took a sip of my tea, but it had already grown cold. I was going to request a new one, but the server was already removing the cold tea and replacing it with fresh, hot tea. As I ate my cheese and croissant, I stared at the lake. The sky had darkened and it appeared a storm was blowing in.

By the time my crêpes arrived, the storm had arrived and it was snowing heavily. I was concerned about John being out in the storm on the ski slopes. I was hoping he would cancel the skiing and come back to the hotel. Once before, he had stayed to finish skiing when a storm rolled in, and he came home with severe windburn on his face, that bordered on frostbite.

While I sat staring out into the storm, deep in thought, I felt hands on my shoulders and nearly jumped out of my skin. I whirled around to find John behind me. He was laughing and making fun of me as usual. The server saw what he had done, and smiled. I felt my face flush with embarrassment. Oh how I hated it when he did that to me. He could always tell when I was deep in thought, and vulnerable to his surprise attacks.

He took the seat directly opposite me. The server saw him sit down, and promptly brought café. John was predictable; the staff knew he always had café in the morning. The server asked him if he wanted breakfast, but John told him he had eaten at the ski lodge earlier.

I asked John if he had gotten any skiing in, and he told me that he managed about an hour before he saw the storm coming in, and decided to stop for the day. He didn't like skiing during a storm, after the windburn incident.

As we sat sipping our respective drinks, we stared out at the storm. From the looks of it, this would be quite a storm. There would be a lot of fresh powder on the slopes in the morning; the skiing would be excellent.

I asked John if he had anything he needed to do today, and he told me he had already called his office and faxed the necessary papers to close the deal he was currently working on. He suggested we spend some of the day shopping at the quaint stores, which were located close to the hotel, and the rest of the time in our suite enjoying the view, Jacuzzi, and each other.

I saw the twinkling look in his eye, and hoped we would be up for all day lovemaking. John had times when marathon lovemaking was his first priority. We once spent 12 hours in a hotel in Oslo, and John had ejaculated seven times. He wore me out. All I could do was lay there and take it, but I loved every minute of it.

We finished up, and John signed the check. We headed out to the lobby for the elevators, and ran into Jacques at the front desk. John asked if he was well, that we had heard he had trouble sleeping the previous night. Jacques gave us a wink, and told us that he appreciated our interest in his health, and that once he had finally gotten to bed he was able to sleep. All three of us sported large smiles at that remark. To anyone else listening, the exchange was very innocent; to us it was completely wicked.

He asked if we would be in for the day, and John told him we probably would, but wanted to get some shopping done too. He told us that the chambermaids had finished our linen change, and the suite was completely freshened and ready for us. John thanked him and we headed for the elevators once again.

When the elevator doors closed, John pinned me to the wall and grabbed my groin. He lowered his voice, and using his most menacing tone, asked if I was ready for rough sex. Taking on my usual passive role in the rough sex games, I timidly replied to him that I was his sex slave; and he should use me anyway he wanted. With that, he leaned forward and bit me sharply on the neck. The bite was somewhat painful, but caused a rush of erotic feelings to race through me. My knob began to harden.

As the elevator doors opened on our floor, John grabbed my shirt at the neck and dragged me to the suite. Once inside, he pushed me roughly onto the settee. He ordered me to strip out of my clothes. I complied immediately. When he was in one of his rough moods, he usually didn't remove his clothes. I think he felt more powerful with his clothing on.

He told me to get the box of sex accessories from the bedroom. Rough sex was not my most favorite form of sex, but I knew that John needed it on occasion. I think it had something to do with the caveman inside him trying to get out, an alpha male thing. We carried the small box whenever we traveled, especially for these times.

I returned with the box, and John opened it. He took out the handcuffs, and cuffed one of my hands to the arm of the settee. He pushed me down into a sitting position. Next, he took out a thick, studded leather cock ring and forced it around my small pénis and bollocks, cinching it tight enough to cause me pain. He took out the custom molded dildo, cast from his manhood and ordered me to assume the position. I got up on my hands and knees, and felt him pushing the large dildo into my anus without the benefit of lubricant.

On the second push, he was able to get the dildo to pass my sphincter. He then buried it all the way in. When the dildo was in place, he turned me around to face him, and handcuffed my other hand to the settee. With my arms stretched out, I looked crucified.

He quickly lowered his zipper and brought his steel hard organ out of his pants. He allowed me to look at it for a minute, and then he stepped up to my face and proceeded to slap me with it. I opened my mouth and stuck out my tongue hoping to get a taste of him. With only a few slaps, he was already leaking copiously. I could taste the juice as his tool slid across my tongue.

At this point, he ordered me to suck him, and slammed himself into my mouth. With a single thrust, his sausage was down my throat, pushing deeply into me. I commenced using every oral skill I knew, to please and pleasure him. I felt him lean into me. His stomach and abdomen were pushing against my face. He placed his hands on my shoulders, and proceeded to bounce me up and down on the settee. This caused the dildo to slide in and out of my anus in rhythm with the thrusting of his tool in my throat.

I was enjoying myself; the front and back assault at the same time by this powerful man, made me tingle all over. The cock ring had my little pénis rock hard, and I was so wishing I could reach it to rub myself. Damn those handcuffs!

I felt John pulsing and stretching in my throat, and figured he would shoot very soon. To my surprise however, he withdrew from my mouth, released one of the handcuffs, turned me around so he could reach my bottom, and removed the dildo from my anus.

Without a word, he stepped up behind me, forcing his meat into my now stretched anus, and the dildo into my mouth and down my throat. He resumed his ramming speed, and the pulsing and stretching quickly resumed.

He lasted about five more minutes, and then with a loud groan, he stopped, and unloaded in my anus. It was a massive ejaculation, much more than usual. This was common when John was in rough mode. As he slipped out of my anus, he withdrew the dildo from my mouth. It was good to breathe normally again. John retrieved the martinet, a type of small flogging implement, from the box and moved back to me. He also had his black leather gloves with him. He put the martinet on my back, and slowly put his gloves on. Once the gloves were on, the gently rubbed and squeezed my buttocks. The feel of the cool leather on my skin had me as close to shooting as I had since we began.

After several minutes, he picked up the martinet, and began dragging it slowly from my neck to my buttocks. It made me shiver, and goose bumps rose from my skin. He moved to the side of me, and by turning my head, I was able to see him.

He stood taking several practice swings with the martinet, and with each swing, his organ got closer to busting at the seams. I thought it would explode from his body if he didn't hurry and finish. Juice was running in a non-stop stream from the head to the floor.

Finally, he was ready to begin, and I tried to relax all of my muscles, knowing that the pain would lessen if I did. I heard John take in a deep breath, and then heard the swing of the martinet just as it struck my naked buttocks. I heard the slap on my skin before I felt the first rush of pain. With the pain, came the overwhelming sense of pleasure. My small pénis engorged as far as it could go without rupturing.

By the time I felt the pleasure starting to wane, the martinet struck a second time, causing the same reaction. John swung the martinet ten times, with the final blow causing me a massive ejaculation all over the settee. Once I started to shoot, I just kept shooting.

As I began shooting, John slammed his incredibly stiff rod into me and began shooting. Considering he had just unloaded a full load, I was surprised at the amount of semen shooting into me. Once done, he withdrew, and I could feel his semen running out of me and onto the settee. John sat down to catch his breath, and continued rubbing my now well-spanked bottom with his leather glove. He released one handcuff, and turned me around. He handed me a small towel to put down over the puddles of semen on the settee.

He gripped my hips with his hands and pivoted me around so I could sit down. He looked at my swollen member, and commented on how large it looked. This was his way of complimenting me on my size, even though we both knew how small I really was.

He reached for me, massaged the head with his gloved fingertips, and slowly stroked me. The feel of the leather rubbing against the head was indescribable. He then did the unexpected. He knelt down in front of me and kissed my little tool. John rarely engaged in oral sex with me or anyone else. He proceeded to fellate me and I could not control myself. After just a few moments, I started to swell and pulse. I thought that after the spanking orgasm, I would be done for a while, but I realised that another orgasm was beginning. John didn't take semen in his mouth, so I told him I was about to shoot. He sat back up and continued pumping me with his hand. I climaxed very hard, shooting semen up into the air, which then splashed down on John's gloved hand and my belly.

As my breathing returned to normal, John removed the handcuffs and put them back into the toy box. He released the cock ring, and placed it in the box. He left the dildo out on the table so I could wash it before putting it away.

With the handcuffs off, I was able to rub my wrists, which had become sore from the cuffing. John took my face between his hands and gave me one of his most passionate kisses, which he gave as a reward, only after rough sex.

He took me by the hand and walked me to the bathroom, where he started the Jacuzzi running, and opened a bottle of chilled Champagne that was in the wine cooler. He realised that my muscles were sometimes sore after rough sex and a warm bath helped to relax them. He smiled and told me he had arranged it with Jacques while we were at breakfast.

As I climbed into the tub, he poured the wine and handed me a glass. As I settled into the tub, I felt the hot water splash on my now freshly spanked, striped buttocks, and it burned just a little. The pain was enough to cause me another erection; apparently, I liked the pain more that I wanted to admit. Then I thought of the famous quote by the Marquis De Sade, "It is always by way of pain one arrives at pleasure".

Once I settled in the tub, John turned on the shower and stepped in.

Chapter 12

When I saw John getting out of the shower, I quickly finished my Champagne and got out of the tub. We stood facing each other while we dried off. John tossed his towel on the floor and reached for one of the robes. He slipped into it, and reached for a second for me. I put my towel on the edge of the marble vanity, and got into the robe John was holding open for me. Once in the robe, I reached down to pick up John's towel, and put it with mine. He laughed and reminded me that the hotel paid people to clean up after us.

I gave him my harshest look, and reminded him that the staff did an outstanding job keeping our suite spotless, and that he did not need to cause them extra work. He just smiled at me and pushed both towels onto the floor. Sometimes he could be so exasperating. I left both of the towels on the floor, not wanting to provoke John to anger. We went into the bedroom to dress, and I asked John where he planned on going so that I could dress appropriately.

He told me he wanted to have lunch at La Marmite. He liked riding the inclined railroad up the mountain to the restaurant, and the food was always excellent. The magnificent view from the mountain was spectacular. I reminded him that there was a powerful winter storm outside and we would probably have difficulty getting up the mountain to the restaurant. He decided we would go to Café Hanselmann instead. He called Jacques and asked him to have the hotel car readied for us.

We dressed in casual après skiwear, wanting to keep warm from the storm outside. Once dressed, we made our way to the lobby.

Jacques was in the lobby waiting for us and I could see that the car was already out front waiting for us. He escorted us to the front door and turned our care over to the driver, who was standing ready to open the car door for us. He wished us bon appetite, and closed the hotel door.

The driver opened the door, and we quickly got into the vehicle. The wind was blowing quite hard, swirling snow all around the entrance of the hotel. Once inside, the driver confirmed that we did indeed want to go to Café Hanselmann. John told him that we did and the car headed out to the street.

As the car pulled out onto the street, I was able to see that the wind was driving the snow fiercely across the street. I asked the driver if it was safe for him to drive, and he told us he had driven here all his life, and this was not a traffic-stopping storm.

When we pulled up to the restaurant, the doorman immediately came out to open the door for us. As we exited the vehicle, John attempted to provide a gratuity to the driver, but he shook his head and told us he would be waiting for us when we had finished our lunch. Apparently, Jacques had told him not to leave us at the restaurant.

As we entered, it became obvious that the restaurant was dated. The furniture and wall coverings gave away their age. John saw me looking, and remarked that the charm of the place outweighed the dated décor.

Though the dining room was crowded, the maître d' immediately seated us at a secluded table near the fireplace. Our server met us at the table and offered to help us get out of our overstuffed jackets. After shedding our jackets, the server told us he would return with our apèritif. In moments, he was back with two glasses of Pernod and a small ornate pitcher of ice water. He asked how we preferred it, and John told him two to one. He quickly mixed the liquids, and departed, leaving menus for us.

We sipped the Pernod, and looked over the menu. John decided on the steak, of course. I chose the pâté au poulet, a type of chicken potpie. We chatted while we waited for our meals. John told me that the restaurant was over a hundred years old, and the original family that opened it, still owned it.

Once served, we quickly ate our lunch and passed on dessert. John called for the cheque, and signed it after adding an appropriate gratuity.

We donned our jackets and made our way to the door. As the doorman opened the door, the car was pulling up in front. The driver got out and quickly opened the door for us and we slid in. The interior of the car was warm, and we made the short drive back to the hotel quite quickly.

Once at the hotel, the doorman was waiting to open the car door for us. As we exited the car, John provided a nice gratuity to the driver and thanked him for waiting for us at the restaurant.

We wasted no time in getting into the lobby. The outside temperature seemed to be much colder than when we left for lunch. Jacques met us at the elevator, and enquired about our lunch. John told him that it was quite nice, but the steak was not as tender as he expected. I told him my chicken was very nice and I had no complaints. Jacques asked if we were in for the rest of the day, and John told him that we were, as it was too cold to go shopping. We boarded the elevator and pushed the button for our floor. Once we arrived, we exited and headed for our suite.

John opened the door for me, and we went in. The chambermaids had been in, and the suite had fresh cut flowers in several crystal vases. The bearskin rug was clean, without a trace of sperm remaining on it. Jacques had placed a bottle of Champagne in an ice bucket, and a bottle of A. H. Hirsch Reserve Bourbon on a silver tray. I poured the bourbon over some ice for John, before pouring the Champagne for myself.

Jacques had set the fire for us, and it was blazing delightfully, pouring warmth into the room. John sat down on the settee, and pulled off his boots. As he sat sipping his drink, I sat down next to him and pulled off my boots.

Once I was comfortable, John put his arm around my neck and

pulled me to him. He playfully kissed me, and I was able to taste the bourbon on his lips. I always enjoyed the flavour of bourbon from John's lips. I put down my wine, and slipped my hand up under his sweater. I moved up his stomach to his chest and started to massage his nipples. While I massaged him, I looked down and saw movement in his pants. Obviously, he liked the massage and his organ was rapidly becoming erect.

As I worked on him, he began kissing me more seriously, driving his tongue into my mouth. I enjoyed him kissing me this way, as I enjoyed him dominating me. I let my hand slide down into his pants, and grasped his tool firmly. I provided some minor stroking, while working his belt from his pants. Once I had the belt off, I was able to get both of my hands on his hips and pull his pants downward. He helped my lifting his buttocks. I pulled his pants all the way to the floor and slipped them off his feet.

With him, naked from the waist down, I wasted no time in getting my tongue working on his manhood. I retracted his foreskin, and began licking him from his bollocks to the tip of his phallus. I first sucked each of his bollocks into my mouth and provided them with a tongue massage. Once done, I moved up his shaft, licking and nibbling as I went. He always liked having his frenum played with, so when I reached it, I nipped at it gently with my teeth, pulling on the skin. My immediate reward was a string of juice leaking from the head. I licked it, and followed the string to the opening in the head.

I drove my tongue as far into it as I could, and John's hips instinctively rose up, driving my tongue even farther into him. After a few more licks, I opened my mouth wide and forced him into my mouth and down my throat in one continuous slide. He moaned loudly as the sensations washed over him. In moments, his pubes engulfed my nose, and my tongue was once again licking his bollocks. I held him tightly in my throat, letting the muscles work on him, before starting the usual up and down motion. After only a few minutes, he pulled himself from my mouth and stood up.

He pulled off his sweater and shirt, and stood before me completely naked. He pulled me to my feet, and told me to strip out of my clothes. I wasted no time complying with his command. In a flash, we were both completely naked.

Next, he directed me to take the hands and knees position on the white rug in front of the fireplace. As he moved to get behind me, he stopped at one of the trays that Jacques had put condoms on, and grabbed a small tube of lube.

Once he was behind me, he put both his hands on both of my inner thighs, and spread my legs as far apart as they would go. He then put some of the lube on my tunnel and massaged it in deeply. Next, it was two fingers I felt inside me, then three. When he pulled his fingers from me, I spread my legs again as far as they would go. I expected him to mount and penetrate me, but instead he took time to slap and spank both of my buttocks. The sting I felt with each slap caused my sexual excitement to soar. I enjoyed an occasional spanking, just because John took such pleasure from spanking me. My small pénis was hard and throbbing from the spanking I was receiving. After about ten slaps to each cheek, I felt him spreading lube on both warm and reddened cheeks. I wondered why the spanking has been of such short duration. Usually when John spanked me, it was for long enough to bring me to tears.

I next felt the head of his tool against the tightness of my anus. With only minor slowing, he drove his entire shaft into me. In seconds, I felt the wonderful fullness of having him inside me. His abdomen made contact with my cheeks, and he started a side-to-side circular motion. Now I understood why he lubed my cheeks. It was a lovely sensation, his abdomen sliding and circling my freshly spanked cheeks.

Once done with the preliminaries, I felt him fully mount me, his chest on my back. He slid his arms up my sides, under my armpits, and across my chest, and finally locked his hands behind my neck. He had effectively pinned me to the floor.

I heard him take in several deep breaths, and the next thing I knew, he was pounding into me like a jackhammer. With his hands behind my neck, he forced my head to the floor, causing my buttocks to rise up. This gave him even greater advantage with which to pound me. I felt his bollocks slapping roughly against me, and I thought he must have been hurting himself, judging from the force with which his bollocks were slapping me. As the pounding intensified, I heard him begin to groan and pant heavily. His speed increased, and he continued to push as deeply as he could into me.

=oOo=

After just a few minutes more, I felt him increase to jack rabbit speed. When his breaths were in short staccato bursts, he growled and made one final mammoth plunge into me as his burning hot semen flooded into my well-serviced rectum. As he exploded, he leaned forward and bit down fiercely on my neck. The pain I felt only intensified my pleasure. Shot after shot of his male juice fired into me, splashing on the walls of my warm, moist tunnel. While still firing, he pulled me from the floor to my knees so we were both kneeling upright. He had unlocked his hands from my neck, and placed them across my chest, forcing my back against his chest.

When he finished shooting, he released my neck from his teeth and slid his hand down to my now swollen and engorged pénis. He slipped his hand around my small tool and started masturbating me. Instead of pulling his hose from me, I felt him start a rhythm that matched the rhythm he was using to masturbate me. I loved feeling his manhood striking my prostate, as his hand stroked me. My level of excitement was unbelievable, and I was only able to last a couple of minutes before my body got the best of me. I felt the semen rushing up my shaft and with a groan, I released the pent up semen. I shot five or six times, each shot firing into the air before landing on John's hand, or on the rug.

John held me tightly while my orgasm completed. Once I was finished, he turned my head towards him and kissed me passionately. As I returned the kiss, I felt him pulling his tool from me. I tried as hard as I could to clamp my anus closed, to prevent the loss of John's semen. There was so much in me, that some leaked out, running down my bollocks and thighs.

John got up from the floor and as he helped me to my feet, he ran his semen-coated hand across my lips and fed it to me.

We made our way to the bathroom, and John started the shower. As the warm water rained down on us, I released my clinched anus and allowed John's semen to escape from me. I could feel the warm water washing away the semen.

Chapter 13

Once out of the shower, I dried John with one of the sumptuous Egyptian cotton towels the hotel provided. I dried his hair and torso, and took an extra moment to dry under his foreskin and bollocks. After that, I dried his legs and feet. He went into the bedroom to dress, and I finished drying myself.

As I went into the bedroom, I saw that John was on his phone, and using his gruffest, most authoritarian tone with the caller. John did not normally take work related phone calls while on vacation with me, so I knew that something serious was brewing.

I grabbed one of the robes, and slipped into it.

He listened to his caller for a minute, and then directed him to meet him in the bar of the hotel in 30 minutes.

I knew better than to pry into John's business, so I kept my mouth shut while inside I was screaming "Tell me, Tell me". I did so want to know what was going on.

John switched off the phone and returned it to his pocket. He apologized for having to interrupt our time together. He then added that his immediate attention was required to resolve a business matter that simply couldn't wait.

He then, most uncharacteristically, looked at me and told me that the CEO of the company he had just bought out was trying to change the terms of the agreement. He told John if he didn't agree, he wouldn't sign the contract.

John's face took on a most menacing look, and he told me he would, "Take care of this little weasel." For an instant, I felt sorry for the weasel, knowing that John would soon tear him to shreds.

John immediately began to undress, and I went to the closet to assist him getting the clothes he needed for this meeting. John's dress indicated the tone of any business meeting he was going to have, as well as how flexible he would be.

I asked him which shirt and tie he wanted, and he indicated the white silk shirt and the black silk tie. I then asked which suit, and he told me he wanted the black Armani suit, black hose, and his black Armani Italian wingtip shoes, then he went back into the bathroom to shave. I quickly gathered his clothes and laid them out on the bed.

When I retrieved his shoes from the closet, I noticed some scuff marks on them. I called Jacques and told him I needed John's shoes polished, dressed, and back to me in 15 minutes. In a flash, the chambermaid was at the door to pick them up.

John finished shaving, and came back to the bedroom wearing only black silk boxers. I helped him into his shirt, and buttoned him in. I put his gold cufflinks into place and secured them. Next, I draped the tie around his neck and knotted it in his usual double Windsor. Then I assisted him into his slacks. He chose a black leather belt with a bright gold buckle designed with his company's logo. I got the belt on him and fastened. I asked him to sit on the bed so I could get his black hose on, while praying that the shoes would arrive in the next two minutes. As I finished up with his hose, Jacques knocked at the door, let himself in, and handed me the freshly dressed shoes. The shine was magnificent. I got the shoes on him and tied.

He stood and walked to the floor length mirrors in the dressing area and reviewed his appearance. He nodded approvingly and thanked me for my help.

When he turned around, he had the most menacing appearance I had ever seen on him. I had never seen him in this particular business attire before. It was obvious that this manner of dress was to frighten and intimidate an opponent. Quite honestly, it frightened me.

I saw Jacques looking at him, but he was speechless, saying nothing.

John nodded at Jacques, kissed me lightly on the cheek, and told me he would return in less than an hour. He also asked me not to go into the bar while he was there, conducting his meeting. I told him I would of course remain in the suite until he returned. With that, John turned on his heel and exited out the door.

Jacques and I just stood looking at each other. All I could think of was that I was glad I was not the man John was going to meet.

I sat down on the settee, and Jacques poured me a glass of chilled wine. As I slowly sipped it, Jacques asked what was going on, and I told him simply that John was going to a meeting to destroy a business associate. He looked at me, and quietly let himself out.

I moved over in front of the fireplace and sat down on the soft rug. The fire was quite small, and provided little heat to the room. I thought about calling the reception desk, but decided against it. I was in no mood to have one of the maintenance staff in the room seeing to the fire. That would have meant getting up and putting on some clothes. I was very comfortable in the robe and intended to stay that way.

I got my wine flute and sat staring at the dying fire. My mind was racing, attempting to digest the incident I had just experienced with John. While sitting, deeply in thought, I heard the passkey in the door. Jacques came into the room with a maintenance cart in tow, covered with a corduroy drape emblazoned with the hotel crest.

Jacques looked over at me and told me he had knocked several times, but I had not responded. Since he knew I was alone in the room, he had used his passkey.

He pushed the cart over to the fireplace, removed the drape, and unloaded the wood hidden under it. He stacked it neatly on both sides of the fireplace. He then set to work rebuilding the fire. In no time at all, the fire was once again cheerfully blazing, filling the room with its delightful heat.

When he finished, Jacques asked if we were staying in for dinner, or eating at the restaurant. If we were dining out, he would make us a reservation. I explained that I had never seen John like this and had no idea what to do. He smiled at me and told me he would go ahead and make the reservation in the hotel restaurant just in case. I thanked him for rebuilding the fire, and for making a dinner reservation for us. I allowed my gaze to return to the fire. From behind me, I heard Jacques let himself out.

A short time later, I heard a key in the lock, and looked over to see John letting himself into the suite. The scowl and menacing look were no longer on his face, but he was not smiling. He made his way over to me, and when he reached me, he grabbed the back of the robe and pulled me to my feet. I did not know how to react, and while I was deciding what to do, John kissed me passionately on the lips and neck. When he was finished kissing me, he dropped me gently to the floor.

He stood next to me, and started stripping out of his clothes, letting them fall to the floor is a disheveled pile. Once naked, he headed to the shower. He called back to me to have every piece of clothing cleaned, as he could not stand the smell of vermin on his clothing.

I called down to the reception desk and requested immediate laundry service. As I hung up the telephone, I could hear John starting the water in the shower. In a matter of a couple of minutes, there was a knock on the door. I pulled my robe up around me and answered the door. Standing there was a delightful looking young man, dressed in a hotel uniform. He told me he was from the laundry to pick up some articles of clothing for cleaning. He had a plastic laundry bag with him, so I directed him to the pile of clothes on the floor. He scooped them up, asked when they needed to be back, and headed to the door. I told him I would like to have the clothes back first thing in the morning. He indicated that he understood, and went out the door. It was only after I turned around and headed back to the fire that I realised my robe had been partially open and my pénis had been on display for the laundry boy to see. I hoped I had not offended him.

Just after the laundry boy had departed, John came into the living room wearing his shower robe. He neglected to tie it around his waist. His skin was still wet from his chest to his feet. I so loved his beautiful body. His pénis was semi-erect, with the foreskin just starting to retract. He looked hungrily at me, and drew closer. I rose up on my knees, anticipating his need for oral sex. When he finally reached me, he took hold of his maleness, completely retracted the foreskin, and proceeded to rub the head across my lips. This action left no question as to what he wanted.

Rather than play on my tongue, he forcefully guided his now completely erect tool into my open mouth. He pushed until his bollocks were against my chin. He held himself there for a few moments, making grunting noises. Realising that I needed to breathe, he withdrew from my throat, but kept the head in my mouth.

After a brief chance to catch my breath, he began a near frantic pounding of my mouth and throat. I felt him stretching and pulsing, and quickly thought that he might prematurely ejaculate. John rarely lost control of his ejaculation, so I was most surprised when he did in fact begin shooting his semen down my throat and filling my mouth. I took his load as I always did, swallowing in time with his pumping. I prided myself on not losing a drop of semen from my lips.

Once his ejaculation concluded, I continued to gently suck and tease him. He did not withdraw immediately, instead letting me play with him for a few minutes. He took longer than usual to soften, but once he was completely soft he slowly withdrew. As he backed away from me, I cleaned him up the best I could.

Once he sat down on the settee, he apologized for prematurely ejaculating, explaining that whenever he had to harshly deal, or destroy a business associate, he almost always shot his load too soon. He explained that he did not usually engage in sex with a partner after these types of negative encounters, preferring to masturbate privately. He told me that he believed it had something to do with being an alpha male.

He extended his hands to me, and helped me up from the floor. I sat down next to him on the settee, snuggling next to him while he wrapped his arm around my shoulder. We pulled our robes up to our necks, not in modesty, but for comfort. The room was once again cooling and the fire needed tending to. I reached for the telephone, and called the front desk to request assistance with our fire.

We sat looking out the French doors onto the balcony enjoying the view. I then realised that the storm had blown itself out and the snow had stopped falling. The moonlight reflected brilliantly in the freshly fallen snow, giving everything an ethereal look. As we sat there, he leaned into me and gave me one of his most passionate kisses. At that moment, I felt incredibly sheltered, and loved.

I asked John if he wanted to dress and go to dinner, or if he preferred to order in. He looked over at me, and with a smile told me, he wanted to have dinner, in the suite tonight.

Chapter 14

I left John on the settee looking out into the night. I asked what he would prefer for dinner, and he told me to order what I wanted.

I made my way to the phone, first calling room service to order dinner and second calling Jacques to come and tend to the fire. Room service asked if our usual Châteaubriand dinner would be acceptable and I told them it would be fine.

The front desk did not know where Jacques was at the minute, and I asked if someone else could help. I explained that the fire was dying in our suite, and that I knew nothing about getting it blazing again. The clerk told me he would dispatch one of the maintenance men to take care of it for me.

On my way back to the settee, I stopped at the bar to make drinks for John and me. I asked him if bourbon was would be his drink of choice for the evening, and he indicated that it would. I poured his bourbon into a glass and added ice. I then found a nice bottle of Courvoisier Erte Cognac. I poured a small portion into a snifter, and carried the drinks to the settee.

I handed John his bourbon, and sat down with him. He sipped at his drink while I was still warming the snifter in the palm of my hand. He talked absently mindedly about things in general, commenting on the hotel, the staff, and the weather, as though avoiding the obvious topic.

When I could stand it no longer, I asked him if he had successfully concluded his business. He looked over at me first in anger, and then I saw the noticeable softening of his features. He told me again that he was sorry that his business had interfered with our time together. He then looked me straight in the eyes and asked if I really wanted to know about this side of his business, or was I just being polite. I assured him I was interested in all that he did.

At that moment, there was a knock at the door and I nearly jumped out of my skin, having been so intent on what John had been saying. I got up to answer it, cursing whoever it was. I was about to get the juicy details, and now it would have to wait.

I opened the door to find the maintenance man. He explained that he was here to take care of our fire. I let him in and closed the door behind him. He went immediately to the fireplace and began to rebuild the fire. When he squatted down, his pants drew tightly against him, revealing a nice set of muscular buttocks, with just a hint of cleft showing at the top of his pants. My first thought was that this was a man that John could enjoy mounting. I then realised that I was semi-erect, and my robe was not concealing everything. I attempted to adjust my robe as the maintenance man stood up, having completed caring for the fire.

As he turned towards me, he adjusted his pants and I was able to discern a lengthy, meaty bulge in the front of his pants. As I walked him to the door, I saw him checking out both of us. As my robe was slightly open, he had a peek at the head of my small, circumcised pénis and my bollocks. As I let him out the door, I told him he was welcome to come back later that evening for drinks. He smiled knowingly, and nodded his head affirmatively.

I quickly returned my attention to John and made my way back to the settee. John had finished his drink and I took the empty glass back to the bar to refill it. I poured him another drink, and picked up the Cognac I had left sitting on the bar when I answered the door.

Once seated next to John, he continued our previous conversation. He explained that the man he had met in the bar was reneging on a contract they had agreed on several weeks ago, and was refusing to finalize the contract. He told me that this happened very rarely in his business and upset him greatly. I asked if the meeting had played out as he expected. He said yes. I then asked how he managed it. He told me that when first negotiating the contract, he had his doubts about this man and his willingness to complete the contract. As insurance against such an event, he had booked the man into an excellent local hotel and invited him to stay overnight before returning home.

At first, the man protested, explaining his wife and children were expecting him home immediately. John reminded him that if he left now, his flight would arrive home in the middle of the night, and he would end up waking his family. The man finally agreed, and John told him he had set up an open account at the hotel, and he need not worry about paying for anything. With that, John sent the man off in a chauffeured company car to the hotel.

Once at the hotel, the man went straight to the bar and began drinking. He got very friendly with two prostitutes he found there. Of course, John had arranged for them to be there. The man invited them to his room and they accepted. A fun filled night of lewd and lascivious sex ensued, with a photographer recording all the fun.

John had merely shown the pictures to the man and indicated he would have them delivered to his wife and daughters the next day, if the contract wasn't signed immediately. Of course, the man signed the contract. John told him copies of the pictures were in his lawyer's office, and if the man attempted to sabotage the deal, he would be sending them to his house as well as the local newspapers the next day. With that out of the way, he sent the man on his way to Berlin.

John told me he did not normally do business this way, and it made him feel "dirty". His business philosophy was to treat everyone fairly and with respect. I wrapped my arms around his neck and kissed him passionately. I then whispered in his ear that I would have done the same thing. I also asked him to put the incident behind him now, so our time together could return to a happy note. I also informed him about the invitation I had extended to the maintenance man. He smiled and rubbed the front of his robe.

I put my Cognac down on the table, and snuggled up to John. He allowed my hands to caress his chest through the thick material of his robe. As his ardor began to increase, he threw back his head, which caused his robe to open to the waist.

As he lay back, my hands worked their way to his nipples and began a gentle circular massage of the hard little nubs. I leaned forward and began planting sweet kisses on the sides of his neck. I was working my way down to his nipples when he gently pushed me down on my back on the seat cushions of the settee. He quickly sandwiched me between the cushions and his chest. He loved the power he felt when he kept me in a missionary position. He covered my mouth with his, as he provided me once again one of his most passionate kisses. As he continued kissing me, I reached down to his waist and untied the cord that was holding the robe closed. His robe immediately fell open, exposing all of him.

I reached lower, and began a soft and gently massage of his bollocks and pénis. I slowly slid his foreskin up and down the rigid shaft and I felt him breathing slightly faster into my mouth. As he released me from the kiss, he turned me around so that my chest was against the back of the settee. I knew his intent, so I lifted my backside to a suitable height to allow him to penetrate me. He paused for a moment, while he located the tube of sensual oil that he had put into his robe pocket earlier.

Once he had the oil out, he moved closer to me and poured a small amount of it into my cleft. He gently massaged it in until he reached my anus and slipped his fingers into me one at a time. As his fingers entered me, I felt my sphincter clamp down on them. He paused for a moment, and then began the familiar in and out motion with his fingers. He massaged my prostate until I was writhing on the settee. I was humping the back of the settee, whenever John's fingers pushed me far enough forward for my pénis to make contact with it.

I started begging him to mount me. I needed him inside me desperately. Finally, he gave in to my begging, mounting me and inserting all of his manhood into me in a single thrust. He held me tightly around the waist as he pummeled me. It felt like his pénis was banging on my navel, struggling to get out.

The sheer speed and depth of penetration caused me to orgasm, shooting my seed onto the back of the settee. Simultaneously, my sphincter clamped down on John like a vice, causing him to go over the top. I felt his warm semen shooting into me. There was so much semen shooting into me, that it started leaking out of me before John pulled out.

Once John withdrew from me, I turned and collapsed on the settee. John joined me, sitting by my side, catching his breath. While he still had the glazed after look, I used my robe to clean him up, and attempted to wipe the sperm from the settee. I knew that after an orgasm like that, he would be too sensitive for even my soft lips.

As we lay back recovering, there was a soft knock at the door. A man's voice announced that room service had arrived. I pulled my robe closed around me, and covered John with his. I then made my way to the door and opened it, allowing the server to bring dinner in on a silver cart.

It took the server no time at all to set up dinner for us. When everything was set, he announced that dinner was prepared and asked if we needed him to do anything else for us. When I responded no, he turned and quietly made his way to the door, letting himself out.

Dinner was pleasant, the steak perfectly cooked. The oven roasted Château potatoes were buttery, and well seasoned, while the honey glazed, carrots were delightful.

After dinner, John joined me in the bath, and he allowed me to wash him. When we got out of the tub, I dried him off and offered him a clean robe to wear. He refused the robe and made his way to the bedroom. Once seated on the bed, he invited me to sit with him.

We talked for a few minutes and then John announced he was ready for bed. I turned the bed down, and slipped under the goose down duvet. John joined me a moment later, spooning up against my back.

I could feel his erection rubbing against me, and thought to myself how can he be ready for another round? As he spooned me, I lifted my leg and he slipped his pénis between my thighs. I was quite surprised, as I expected him to penetrate me. He settled himself in, and slowly thrust himself between my thighs. Within moments, I heard him begin to snore. I pulled his arm up over me and turned out the light.

I gave a fleeting thought to the fact that our vacation was quickly reaching its' conclusion, but did not dwell on that fact. I felt myself slowly slipping into twilight sleep, as the world around me disappeared into the darkness.

Chapter 15

The muffled removal of last night's dinner cart woke me. The sun was peeking into the bedroom from between the drapes, casting small sunbeams across the floor. I felt John's hardness still between my thighs.

Looking out through the semi-open bedroom door, I caught glimpses of the chambermaid cleaning and tidying the living area. I saw Jacques directing the staff in the completion of their individual duties. Fresh cut flowers added a new freshness to the suite, their sweet scent wafting through the suite. The maintenance man was resetting the fireplace, which was now cheerfully crackling.

I looked over at our dressing table, and I saw that new robes and slippers and already been put out for us. I got up slowly, allowing John's hardness to slip from between my thighs and slipped into one of the robes. John had turned on his side, and was continuing to sleep.

As I walked out to the living room, the staff warmly greeted me. Jacques asked if they had made too much noise, and I assured him they had not. I told him we had turned in early last night, so I was up early.

Jacques asked if he should order up a breakfast cart, or just a juice and café cart. I thought about it for a minute, and asked him for the juice and café carte. I also asked if he could get us an early lunch reservation at Corviglia Brasserie, since it appeared that John was going to sleep through breakfast. He told me he would take care of it, and was instantly on the phone making the arrangements.

As Jacques hung up his phone, he told me that he had ordered the café cart, and Corviglia Brasserie had confirmed our reservation. I smiled and thanked him for his assistance. With that, he turned and sent all the staff out of the room. He then let himself out.

I moved over to the fireplace, and sat down on the rug. I untied my robe and opened it, allowing the fire to warm my chest, legs and genitals.

My mind was wandering when I heard a knock at the door. I quickly covered myself. I then quietly called out for the visitor to come in. The door swung wide open and the server brought in the café cart. He was a handsome young man, probably Suisse, and very fit.

He rolled the cart over to where I was sitting, and proceeded to set it up for me. In addition to the café, my favorite hot chocolate and orange juice was also on the cart. Additionally, chocolate topped croissants and éclairs decorated the plate.

He poured the hot chocolate for me, and handed me the cup and saucer. I could see his eyes taking in all of me as he looked down. I stretched my leg out, causing the robe to slip away, revealing my small pénis. I was semi-hard, my pénis lolling against the side of my leg. As he gazed at me, I saw him sprout an erection of his own. He appeared to be moderately well hung.

I enquired what his name was, and he told me it was Yves. I then asked if his shift was starting or ending, and he replied with a smile that his shift was over.

We engaged in some minor conversation, and I learned that he was also a student working to pay his college tuition. I assured him that I understood how that was, having done the same myself.

I smiled back, reached up, grasped his zipper between my fingers, and quickly pulled it down. He wore nothing under his uniform pants, which allowed his maleness to spring out, nearly slapping me in the face.

His manhood was of respectable size, I was guessing 6.5 inches. His foreskin partially covered his glans, leaving more than half of it uncovered. He sported a Prince Albert piercing; I guessed it to be about an eight gauge. I reached for his velvety hardness, wrapping my hand easily around his girth. I slowly retracted his foreskin, attempting to judge how far I could pull it back without causing pain to his piercing. As I examined his piercing, I saw that his piercing went through the left side of his foreskin. His frenum, cut in several places, allowed pulling without pain during sex.

Once his foreskin fully retracted, I moved forward to take his maleness into my mouth. The first thing I noticed was the coolness of the metal on my lips. I allowed him to slip all the way inside my mouth, and I used my tongue to rotate his ring through his piercing. As the metal slid through him, a loud moan escaped his lips. I continued to work on the tip, rotating the ring frequently. Very quickly, I found that he was leaking copious amounts of juice from his slit as well as the piercing hole in the underneath side. I used my tongue to spread his juice down his shaft and on to his bollocks. As my tongue lapped his scrotum, he began to plead with me to suck his bollocks. I had just begun working on them, when from the corner of my eye I saw John approaching from the bedroom.

From my vantage point, I was able to see that John was completely erect, with his foreskin already drawn back. He put his finger to his lips, signaling me to remain silent while he slipped up behind Yves. Once behind him, he gave Yves a resounding slap on his buttocks, which resulted in a reflex action on Yves part, forcing all of his pénis down my throat at once, and cutting off my air supply.

As soon as he recovered from the shock of the slap, he jerked his pole from my throat so I was once again able to breathe. He turned to look at John, and he saw that John had a large smile on his face.

John invited him to continue feeding me his hardness, telling him the trade off was that he was going to be penetrating him. Yves thought about it for a minute, assessing the size of John's manliness, then looked at John and finally agreed to the trade.

Yves returned his erection to my mouth, and I was able to feel John bending him over at the waist. This caused his hardness to slide farther into my mouth. I heard Yves make several deep grunting sounds, and I was sure that John was wasting no time penetrating him.

Without any warning, Yves started the traditional push and pull of oral sex. After a moment, I realized that his motions resulted from John impaling him repeatedly. I continued working on Yves' pénis, and very shortly, he grabbed the back of my head, pulled me him, buried his manhood deeply into me and blew his load of sperm directly down my throat. When he pulled back, I found myself enjoying the taste of his fresh young semen, allowing it to roll around in my mouth. I expected Yves to withdraw from me, but he suddenly began thrusting again. I realized that John must still be impaling him, and soon I heard the grunting noises John makes when he fills another man with his seed.

After a few moments, Yves withdrew from my mouth, and John withdrew from Yves' anus. I still had my full erection, awaiting my satisfaction. John noticed my condition and signaled me to come over next to him.

When I got next to him, he bent Yves over the arm of the settee, and spread his cheeks so I was able to see his anus, with John's semen dripping from it. John took hold of my maleness, and dragged me over to Yves. He then told me he wanted me to mount Yves.

I was mortified at the thought, having never done such a thing in my entire life. John pulled me to Yves until the head of my maleness was against his anus. With all of John's semen leaking out, I knew that no extra lube would be required. I really didn't want to penetrate this boy, and John knew it. He reached behind me, and leaned his weight against by buttocks, causing my pénis to force its way into Yves. Yves didn't make a sound.

I felt sure that since my manhood was so small, Yves probably didn't even realize I had penetrated him after taking a pénis as large as John's. Once John pushed me all the way inside of Yves, I simply didn't move. I didn't like the feeling of being inside a man. John seeing and feeling my hesitancy moved up behind me and slipped his erection into me. As he fully penetrated me, I felt my own erection harden. Once John began thrusting into me, I could not help but thrust into Yves.

John took his time with me. I think he thought that if he pounded me long enough, I would shoot my load in Yves. After considerable effort, John shot into me, and I kept my semen to myself.

Yves stood up and asked me if there was a problem causing me not to ejaculate in him. I explained to him I was a dedicated bottom, and topping another man wasn't something I wanted to do.

Yves went to the bathroom, cleaned up and returned looking as if nothing had happened. He thanked us both for the adventure, and hoped he would see us again. We assured him that we would see him again before we finished our vacation. With that, he let himself out of the suite.

I was sitting nude on the settee, when John came over and sat next to me. He explained that he was sure I wanted to occasionally top, but thought I might think of that as cheating on him. I told him that topping a man was not on my list of things to do.

I explained to him that all my life I was a bottom. My brother first penetrated me when I was six years old and he was 12. He taught me to suck him, and give him hand jobs. Then one night he slipped into my bed, lubed my anus with spit and slid his 3-inch boyhood into me in one quick thrust. It hurt, but I loved it. He pushed and pulled, and rode me like a bucking bronco. He had a dry orgasm while inside me. I felt wonderful feelings but didn't orgasm.

He asked if I would let him do it again, and I told him yes, as long as he sucked me after each episode. On the spot, he rolled me over and gave me my first blowjob. I experienced my first dry orgasm with him. Once I was able to ejaculate, he refused to let me orgasm in his mouth anymore. He said only gay boys took semen in their mouths. He continued riding me, and he would suck me afterwards, but never again did I get to orgasm in his mouth. He always finished me off by hand. Since that time, I have always chosen to be a bottom, servicing well-hung men.

With a look of understanding in his eyes, John reached for me, pulled me to him, and kissed me passionately. He then slipped down my chest and abdomen and took my limp pénis into his mouth. With all of his skills, he brought me to full erection, and proceeded to give me the best blowjob of my life. When I felt myself getting ready to unload, I attempted to pull him off me. I knew he never allowed a man ejaculate in his mouth.

No matter how much I pushed him away from me, he held tight. Finally, I could hold back no longer and shot volley after volley of hot semen directly into his mouth.

Once I had finished shooting my load, John released me, and allowed my manhood to slip from his lips. Once I was out of his mouth, he turned to the side and spit my semen out on his robe. I told him that he didn't have to allow me to shoot in his mouth; I was quite satisfied with his wonderful hand jobs. He smiled at me, and told me that it really wasn't so bad having me ejaculate in his mouth. I smiled back at him, knowing that he was lying, and just shook my head from side to side indicating I didn't believe he would ever allow another man to shoot in his mouth. I said nothing to John, but I was overwhelmed with joy at finally shooting my load in his mouth. Because I knew that he didn't allow men to ejaculate in his mouth, it made me feel incredibly special. I had finally achieved one of my lifetime dreams.

Once our post orgasmic bliss had passed, we both got up and headed for the shower. Once in the shower, I slipped to my knees in order to give John another orgasm. As I tried to take him into my mouth, he drew back, reminding me that we were both looking forward to having lunch at The Brasserie and the car would be here in three-quarters of an hour, to pick us up.

We finished cleaning up, and got out of the shower. As usual, I dried John and sent him to dress before drying myself. As he went into the bedroom to get dressed, he turned to ask me if we were dressing informal or casual.

I told him I thought casual après ski would be fine since the restaurant was part of a ski resort complex. He agreed and started looking through the closet. I joined him, and after watching him stand naked in front of the closet for several minutes, I selected clothes for him and asked him to dress.

We finished dressing, and headed off for the lobby. When the elevator let us off, Jacques was there. He told us there had been a problem with the car, and a new one would be arriving within a quarter-hour. He asked if we wanted to sit in the lobby or the bar to wait for the car. We decided to sit in the lobby.

We moved to the seating area near the lobby entrance, and made ourselves comfortable on the overstuffed leather lounge chairs. As we sat down, the barman appeared with Champagne, which he opened and poured for us.

While we sipped the wine and looked out the lobby doors, the sky was darkening and a wet snow had begun to fall. We had time to finish one glass of wine before the car pulled up to the doors. We got to the lobby doors and the doorman held them for us. The driver of the car was apologizing profusely for the delay, while he held the car door open for us. John assured him it wasn't a problem, that we understood it wasn't his fault. The traffic was moving at a crawl, because the snow was freezing to the road, which meant driving on ice. Our driver was obviously a professional, as he had no problems handling the car.

We arrived nearly one-half hour late for our luncheon reservation, but the maître d' greeted us as if we were on time. He escorted us to our table.

Lunch was delectable, with the star of the meal being the braised rabbit. A delightful sage polenta accompanied the rabbit. We ate quickly, as we could see a huge storm rolling in to St. Moritz. We passed on dessert, and John signed the check.

We headed back to the hotel, but the storm hit just before we got there. The snow was falling so heavily, that the driver couldn't have seen more than a few feet ahead of the car. He assured us he would get us safely back to the hotel. He then added with a laugh, that Rolls Royce's don't have accidents. He told us the trip would take awhile, because the traffic was moving so slow.

I opened the liquor bar, and poured John and I both a snifter of brandy. The brandy didn't help the storm any, but it made the ride more bearable. The driver delivered us safely to the hotel, and after assisting our exit from the car, received a large gratuity from John, along with his thanks for returning us safely to the hotel.

Chapter 16

As Jacques greeted us at the door, he asked if we were staying in the hotel for the evening, and John told him we were. Jacques told us he had taken it upon himself to arrange everything we needed for the sauna and hot tub in the fitness center. John smiled and thanked him, telling him that a sauna would be excellent with the weather outside being as it was.

Jacques escorted us to the elevator and took us to the lower level of the hotel. The men's fitness center was more than adequate, with everything a local gym would have. Jacques led us to the sauna, which he had pre warmed, and told us the hot tub was also ready to go. He reminded us the pool was set at 78°F for our comfort. Multiple large white towels and two robes were on the bench outside the sauna. He asked us if we wanted him to take our clothes up to the suite, and we could wear the robes to get to back upstairs using the private elevator. He assured us no one would see us returning to our suite. John nodded to me and we stripped out of our clothes, and gave them to Jacques. He asked if John wanted the fitness room closed for our personal use, and John told him no, we were not planning to be in the fitness center that long.

John took my hand and we went into the shower to clean off before going into the sauna. The warm spray on my body was very relaxing on top of the half bottle of Champagne I had consumed at lunch. We soaped and rinsed, and went to the sauna. The temperature display was indicating 160°F. The heat was delicious, and soon we were both sweating profusely. John was sitting next to me, with his leg touching mine, and I could feel his sweat rolling off his leg and on to mine.

I always loved the smell of clean sweat on John. It had a magical aroma to it that was very erotic. I found I could not contain myself, and leaned over him, licking the sweat from his chest and nipples. He raised his arms over his head, providing me with full access to his armpits. I licked until I thought my tongue would fall off. The sweet smell of his sweat had caused me to become erect, and when I slid my hand down to his groin, I discovered that he was also hard. Even his pénis was sweating, so I rolled back his foreskin and gave it a bath. After a few moments, he pushed my head away, and told me he wanted to enjoy the hot tub and pool before we progressed any farther in our love play.

We got out of the sauna, and walked over to the hot tub. The water temperature felt cooler, and a temperature check indicated 104°F. We had been in the tub only a few minutes when a young man arrived from the main bar with chilled bottles of Saint Geron bottled water. He had the water in a glacette, keeping it cool, which he placed on a small side table. He opened two bottles for us, and asked if we needed anything else. John told him no, and he went on his way. We finished soaking, and John decided he needed a swim in the pool before we left.

We got out of the hot tub, and made our way to the pool. I sat on the steps with my feet and legs in the water while John swam several laps. Because of the temperature in the hot tub, the pool felt cold to me. We finished up at the pool, and we went back to the sauna. We made a side trip to the shower to rinse off the chlorine from the pool.

After toweling off, John helped me into my robe, and I did the same for him. Jacques had arranged for someone to bring house slippers for us to wear, so we slipped them on. We went over to the lift and got onboard. It only took it a few minutes to get us to our floor. When the lift doors opened, we saw that we were only two doors from our suite. We quickly made our way to our suite.

While we were out, Jacques had the chambermaid, clean and straighten the suite. Fresh towels and robes were hanging from the door hangers. The fire was crackling cheerfully. I asked John if we could order dinner in tonight, and just enjoy each other's company. He was fine with that idea, and told me to order whatever I wanted. He asked that I wait an hour before ordering, so he could finish digesting lunch.

I went directly to the bearskin rug, and sat down, getting as close to the fire as I could. John came over to me, and I took him by the hand and pulled him down onto the rug with me. He stretched out, putting one arm behind his head and neck. I could not wait any longer, and I opened his robe. I took a minute to admire his chiseled body. As I pushed his robe open, I leaned in and kissed him on his warm lips. From there, I slipped down to his nipples and began the teasing fun. Once both nipples were hard, I licked my way down his chest and stomach to his maleness. He was partially hard, and I took him in my hand, drawing back his foreskin. I took him in my mouth, and when I pulled back, he was fully erect.

I was feeling somewhat in control, and I decided I wanted him deep inside me. I wanted to feel his pénis massaging my prostate and then filling me with his hot juice. I rose up on my knees, and maneuvered myself into position over him. I reached back and spread my cheeks, and I felt John take hold of his rod and guide the head to my anus. I was not worried about lube, as John was doing his usual outpouring of precum. When I felt the head in place, I began to sit down on it. As I sat, I slid all the way down his shaft in one quick movement. I soon felt his pubic hair and bollocks against my warm skin.

I remained seated, unmoving, until I felt him begin to thrust. Once he started, I began rising and falling in time with his thrusting. Once he began his steady rhythm, I leaned forward and locked my lips to his. His tongue penetrated my mouth, and he mimicked the thrusting action with his tongue. John was in no hurry, and leisurely made love to me. I loved the feeling of him deep inside me, hitting my prostate with each inward thrust. I was leaking copious amount of precum, which was flowing on to his stomach and into his navel.

I felt his phallus swelling, and knew that soon this lovemaking experience would end. He increased his thrusting speed, and began grunting on his inward thrusts. Soon I heard his sharp intake of breath, and then hot semen was exploding from him, filling the depths of me. I held him tightly while he unloaded.

When he finished, he simply stopped all movement and let

himself rest inside me. He took the opportunity to grasp me in his hand, and brought me to orgasm in just a few strokes. My semen poured out onto his chest and stomach. When I finished shooting, I lay against him, massaging the slippery seed between us. As I felt him soften, I gently lifted myself from him, and began to clean him up. I licked all of my juices from his chest and stomach, and then all of his juices from his tool and sack.

We lay there on the rug enjoying the afterglow for a few minutes, when there was a knock at the door. We heard the master key in the lock as we slipped into our robes.

Jacques had let himself in, bringing a bottle of Bourbon, and a bottle of Champagne. At first, he didn't see us on the rug, but as he walked over to set the bottles down our presence became obvious. He gave us a knowing wink and a smile, and asked how the view was from down there. We all laughed, as I put out my hand for him to assist me up from the floor. Once I was up, he helped John up. We sat on the settee while Jacques poured the bourbon over ice, and cracked the Champagne bottle for me.

Jacques asked if we wanted him to make dinner reservations for us in the hotel restaurant. John replied no, that he wanted to dine in our room tonight. Jacques then asked if we required anything special on the menu, and John told him he wanted Escargots à la Bourguignonne, French bread and whipped butter. I love getting this appetizer at Badrutt's, as the escargots are a local crop and provide a distinct and pleasant earthy flavour. John told him we both would have prime rib with fresh vegetables. He asked Jacques to bring dinner in about an hour.

Once Jacques had left, we got back into our robes and walked over to the French doors. The snow was wet, falling in a heavy curtain and the visibility was minimal. John had his arm around me as we stood looking out. Neither of us spoke, not wanting to break the magic of the romantic moment. John finally broke the silence, and asked what I wanted to do tomorrow, as it would be our last day in St. Moritz. I told him I wanted him to go skiing in the morning, then lunch in the hotel, and the rest of the day in our suite, finding things to amuse ourselves, which was our euphemism for sex. He then asked if I wanted the evening to be just the two of us. I told him I was fine with whatever he wanted, since I would have him all to myself for the trip back to Paris.

Dinner arrived, and we ate by the fireplace in the dining area. We rarely used this part of the suite, but John wanted to eat there tonight. Jacques had lit the room candles as well as the table candles. The escargot was fantastic. The prime rib exceeded our expectations. Dessert was a wonderful pear tarte tatin.

After dinner, we bathed and soaked in the Jacuzzi before retiring to bed. John initiated a slow and gentle lovemaking, and for the evening, his attention centered on my pleasure. He fellated me to a beautiful orgasm, before mounting me and filling me with his warm juice.

Within minutes of dismounting me, he was on his side sleeping. I spent a few minutes looking at his sleeping body, and realising that tomorrow would be our last day of holiday. The thought made me sad, but I also realised that it would only be a few weeks before he would be back and we would be doing this all again.

I heard Jacques let himself in to set the fire for the night. He looked in on us and saw I was awake. He whispered, asking if I needed anything, and I told him no. He came over and adjusted the duvet, said to me, "bonne nuit", then turned and left just as quietly as he had come.

Chapter 17

When I woke, the room was still in darkness, and the clock was displaying 5:30am. I heard the shower running, and assumed that John was getting ready to go skiing. I stretched out my muscles, and allowed myself time to wake up.

As John was coming out of the bathroom in his towel, I turned on the light so he would know I was awake. He moved to my side of the bed, and gave me a nice good morning kiss. I sat up and took his towel from him, so I could dry him off. As I was drying him, Jacques was knocking softly at the door.

He let himself in, pushing a service cart with café, tea, and what looked like croissants and butter. He asked where we wanted the café and tea set up and I told him the living room. He went in that direction, and started setting up.

By this time, I had John completely dry except for his hair, and I got up off the bed, took John by the hand, and led him naked to the living area. I sat him down on the settee, and proceeded to dry his hair. Since he was sitting and I was standing, my pénis was directly in front of his face. He took his hand, and gently slapped it back and forth, so it swung like a pendulum. As I finished his hair, he squeezed my pénis several times.

Jacques had the café and tea poured, and set the cups down in front of us. The liquids were refreshing, and I started to feel alive. Jacques asked if John would like breakfast before leaving for the slopes and John told him no. He said he would only be on the slopes a couple of hours, as it was our last day and he wanted to have breakfast here in the hotel with me, when he got back.

Jacques retrieved John's skiwear from the bedroom closet, and brought it out to the living area. He laid the clothing out on the back of the settee. While he helped John into his thermal undershirt, I held his jock strap so he could step into it. I asked if he wanted the cup and he said yes. I placed the cup in the jock before pulling it all the way up and trapping his bollocks and manhood in it. I then helped him into his thermal underwear. Jacques then assisted him into his tight knitted turtleneck, and accompanying vest. Next was his soft shell jacket. After that, we helped him into his ski pants. I had him sit down on the settee, and I put his thermal socks on both his feet, and slipped his Ugg's on. As he stood, Jacques assisted him into his down ski jacket.

With all the bundling taken care of, I kissed him on the cheek and handed him his goggles. He went to the door and Jacques opened it for him.

Jacques immediately phoned the front desk and told them John was on his way, to make sure the car was at the door. He also told them to reserve a table for breakfast.

He came back over by me, and I invited him to sit down on the settee. He smiled and asked if I always pampered John this way. I assured him I did. John deserved being cared for, as his business was so grueling and stressful. Jacques nodded his head in understanding.

I looked down at myself and realised that I was still naked. I told Jacques I was going to the shower and he was welcome to join me. He told me he would love to, as he had covered the night shift and was nearly exhausted. He would have the next 24 hours off. I asked how his wife felt about those kinds of shifts, and he reminded me she was still in visiting with her Mom in Majorca. I got into the bathroom and started the water. Jacques joined me a minute later, stopping only to strip off his uniform before stepping into the shower with me.

Once he was wet, I took the sea sponges and lathered them with soap. I then used them to wash his neck, back, and all the way to his buttocks before turning him around and washing his chest, stomach, abdomen, and genitals. As I washed his maleness and bollocks, he began to harden. I wanted him fully hard, so I continued washing him with my soapy hands. I stroked his pénis and massaged his bollocks for quite some time, before rinsing him off. I then washed his hair. When I was done, he did the same for me, also causing me to harden. We got out of the shower and dried ourselves off.

I invited him to share the bed with me, so I could help him with his hardness. He said he would, but he asked if John would be okay with this arrangement where he wasn't here. I told him John would understand.

I took him by the hand and led him to the bed, gently pushing him down on it. Once he was fully on the bed, I started using my lips on his nipples. They perked up immediately. I took one in each hand, twirled, and squeezed while my tongue found his armpit. I dragged my tongue across the hair in his armpit, and lapped up to the underneath side of his bicep. He moaned the entire time my tongue was in his armpit. I then moved down to his navel, and drove my tongue as far into it as I could. I licked the skin folds around the opening, and Jacques went wild. His manhood was bouncing up and down, his juices dripping from the head, as I lapped his navel. When I finally began to work on his manhood, he literally shook when I took him in my mouth. I cleaned all the juice from the head, and licked my way down his shaft to his bollocks. I licked his sack for several minutes before taking his bollocks in my mouth.

With his sack in my mouth, I used my teeth, gently nibbling at the skin above where the bollocks sat. I bit down gently and pulled the bollocks down in the sack as far as they would go, then slid my tongue back and forth across the bottom of his sack. He was moaning and writhing, at this point, and his juices were flowing.

I lifted off him, asking if he wanted to finish in my mouth, or would he like to mount me. He responded by telling me he really would like to mount me. I asked if I he wanted me to ride him, or allow him to actually mount me. Between breaths, he said, "I want to mount you."

I got up and moved to the side of the bed so I could reach the condoms and lube. I opened the package and removed the condom, put a bit of lube in the tip of it, and placed the opening over the head. I pulled his foreskin back tight and unrolled the device, covering his entire shaft. After squeezing out all the air bubbles, I returned the foreskin to its normal position. I then turned to the foot of the bed, and presented myself for mounting.

Jacques wasted no time moving into position behind me, and used the tube of lube I had placed next to me, to lube his pénis. He crawled up behind me, and I felt the head touch my anus. He was already breathing rapidly, and I thought he might ejaculate too soon. He pushed the head and several inches of the shaft into me, and stopped all movement. He leaned onto my back and whispered in my ear that he needed a moment to get control of himself. I was pleased with his consideration.

Once he was fully in control, he slowly inserted all of himself into me. He grunted when his bollocks pushed against by buttocks. He again took a moment to collect himself, before he began thrusting. He quickly developed a rhythm of several long, slow strokes, followed by several short, rapid strokes. He made sure to tap my prostate with each inward thrust. I was enjoying our lovemaking. He had my juices flowing. He lasted nearly 10 minutes before I heard the change in his breathing. His thrusting speed increased, and his bollocks began to slap against me. I took the opportunity to start pushing back against his inward thrust and soon he was moaning.

As his speed increased, I felt his hand wrap around my manhood and he began stroking me at full speed. He continued until I felt him plunge deeply into me and stopped all movement. I felt him swell and felt the heat of his semen through the condom. As soon as he finished, he returned to stroking me, and it was only another minute before I was shooting sperm all over the bed sheets.

He remained inside me until he was completely soft, and then withdrew. I turned to face him, and I saw the condom was still on his pénis. I removed it gently, and held it in my hand until I had finished cleaning him up. I raised the open end of the condom to my mouth, and poured his semen in. At that moment, I was grateful that Avanti condoms were polyurethane, not latex, and had no objectionable odor or taste.

Once we fully recovered, Jacques moved to get up. I told him that he was welcome to stay in bed and sleep. I knew John wouldn't mind. He smiled and asked me to close the bedroom door and put up the do not disturb sign on it, so the chambermaids wouldn't walk in and find him in my bed when they came in to clean. I told him I would. I looked back at the bed from the shower, and Jacques was already asleep.

I got up and headed back to the shower for a quick rinse off. When I was dry, I brushed my teeth and rinsed with mouthwash to get rid of the semen smell. I dressed in casual clothes, and made my way to the lobby to sit and wait for John to return for breakfast. He had already been gone for two hours, so I knew he wouldn't be much longer.

=oOo=

When I got off the elevator in the lobby, the concierge told me the lodge had just called and told him John had just left. I seated myself in one of the overstuffed leather chairs to wait. The barman appeared and asked if I wanted something to drink, and I asked for a Mimosa. I figured I had better go easy on the bubbly, or I would be too drunk to enjoy the day with John. I had barely finished the first Mimosa, and started my second, when I saw the car pull up to the lobby doors.

In near unison, the driver and doorman opened their respective doors for John. He palmed some bills into the driver's hand, and thanked him for his service. John smiled at the doorman, who smiled back. No money changed hands, but the doorman knew when we checked out, John would take care of everyone who had provided us with service.

John came over and took me by the hand, pulling me out of my chair and dragging me towards the restaurant. He seemed eager to eat. Once seated, he ordered a full English breakfast for himself. I ordered the French breakfast. With café poured for John and my Mimosa replaced, we relaxed. I asked John how the slopes were, and he said the skiing was excellent.

I asked why he seemed in such a good mood, considering today was our last day, and he told me he saw a Zürich newspaper at the resort. There was a picture of Mr. Schmidt. He was the man who tried backing out of his contract with John. Apparently, Interpol has arrested him in Berlin for attempting to smuggle 50,000 undeclared U.S. dollars into Germany. John was smiling wickedly, and I asked if he had anything to do with it, and he merely said that he always had the last laugh. We ate our breakfast while we talked and enjoyed the view.

After breakfast, John said he wanted to swim a couple of laps in the pool and spend some time in the sauna. He asked if I would join him. I told him I would, we went to the concierge to ask for the key to the fitness room, and pool as it was still too early for them to be open. Henri came over and picked up the key, accompanying us. Once he let us in, he told us he would get our towels and toiletries and return directly.

We wasted no time getting out of our clothes, and while I was sitting on the bench pulling off my pants, John came over. His manhood was in my face, and I assumed he needed attention. As I was about to begin, I smelled fresh sperm on him. I looked up and asked if he really needed attention from me, since he had obviously ejaculated quite recently. He laughed and told me he didn't need my services now, that he had caught the towel boy at the resort showers, and persuaded him to provide him with some fun.

John told me the boy was a first year college student, and a virgin. It was his first year working the resort, and had heard about the man sex that went on. He thought he wanted to try it.

Henri interrupted the story by returning with our towels. He noticed that John was semi hard, as was I. He quickly went about setting up our supplies, and put our bottled water on ice. He asked if he should lock the door as he went out, and John told him no, that we weren't going to need that much privacy.

As we walked to the pool, John continued relating his morning adventure to me. The boy led him to the supply closet, and removed his clothes. John quickly did the same, and bent the boy over one of the warm dryers. He kicked the boys legs as far apart as they would go, and lubed him up with some of the skin lotion they provided to their guests. He then mounted him and started penetrating him. He told the boy to push back and breathe in deeply. As the boy did, John slid all of his maleness into the boy in a single thrust.

The boy cried out and John told him the pain would pass quickly. John was in a hurry to get back to the hotel, so he began long, deep strokes while stroking the boy's pénis. John found the boy's prostate, and proceeded to assault it, causing the boy to start grunting and moaning. John increased his stroking speed on the boy's pole, and soon the boy was unloading his seed on the dryer. The clamping of his sphincter put John over the top and he filled the boy with his semen. John left the boy bent over the dryer, panting.

John showered, dressed and went to the car. I commented that the encounter seemed a little cold and clinical, and John said he wasn't there to make love; he was there to take a boy's virginity and unload his sperm. When he wanted lovemaking, he would come to me. His words made me feel special.

When John was done in the pool, we went to the sauna. We sat for about 15 minutes before John was ready to shower and leave. When we got to the showers, I licked the sweat from John's chest, and sucked on his nipples while he set the water temperature. My licking must have been sensual, as John became fully erect. I asked if I should do something about it, and he said no, I could take care of it when we got to the suite. Once dried, we dressed and made our way to the elevator.

An uneventful trip to our suite ensued, and soon John was slipping the key card into the door lock. As we stepped in, I could see the chambermaids had cleaned the room, putting out fresh flowers as always. I looked to the bedroom, and saw the do not disturb sign was still on the bedroom door. John headed to the bedroom, and had the door open before I had time to tell him about Jacques.

I reached the door just as John opened it. There, sprawled on the bed, was Jacques. He was on his back, and his pénis was fully erect, reaching for the ceiling. John looked at me for an explanation, and I told him about Jacques' 24-hour shift and my invitation to him to stay. With a wily smile, he asked if Jacques needed anything besides a place to sleep, and I explained he was having a problem with one of his body parts and I had helped to solve the problem, while on my hands and knees. John laughed at my euphemism, and said that he would have Jacques repay the favor by helping him in the same way. I asked John not to wake Jacques until room service delivered the café I was about to order.

I went out to the living room, and called the front desk for café, tea, and Mimosas. I sat on the settee and thought about the day ahead. A three way with Jacques before lunch would be nice, and then John could arrange the evening's entertainment, to fit his needs.

I looked out towards the balcony, and though it was bright and sunny, the trees on the mountain were bending in the wind, and the sky was darkening in the distance, a sure sign a storm was on its way. I was looking forward to an evening by the fire, while a snowstorm raged outside. It sounded so romantic.

Chapter 18

In about 20 minutes, room service arrived with the service cart. The smell of fresh café wafted through the air as he rolled the cart into the room. The delivery boy was very cute in his crisp, white uniform. He asked where we wanted the café served, and John told him to set up by the settee. He poured café for John and a Mimosa for me from a large glass pitcher. The bar had also sent up a small lead crystal decanter of excellent Irish whisky, a bowl of brown sugar, and a small bowl of freshly whipped cream. Obviously, whoever was tending bar knew that John loved Irish café. Once setup, he asked if we needed anything else, and when we told him no, he quietly left us to our drinks.

John went over to the balcony doors, and stood staring out at the landscape. He was looking very thoughtful, so I didn't attempt to engage him in conversation. He opened the French doors and walked out onto the balcony, and immediately, I joined him. It was cold, and the wind was blowing down from the mountain. The sky had darkened even more, and I was sure the storm was about to hit.

John turned to me and made a sweeping gesture across the sky, as he said, "Look, St. Moritz is sad; knowing that today is our last day here." This was the first time he had mentioned that we were leaving tomorrow. He took me in his arms, pulled me tightly to him and passionately kissed me. As the kiss broke, I told him that though our time here was brief, our love and adventures were intense; and the memories would keep us going until the next time we returned.

He looked back out over the landscape, and asked me how I wanted to spend our last night in St. Moritz. I told him I was hoping that he would arrange everything and surprise me. He turned back to me, and smiled. Then he said, "Anything?" I nodded my head and repeated, "Anything."

He was about to speak, when Jacques appeared at the door wearing only a robe.

He had obviously just gotten out of the shower and his hair was dripping wet. I moved to the door, pushing Jacques back into the room. I told him it was too cold outside for him to be wet and half-naked on the balcony. As we moved inside, John closed the door behind us.

I moved over to the settee, and asked John if he wanted regular café, or Irish café. He said Irish, and I mixed the brown sugar and cream into the café before adding the Irish whiskey. I handed John his cup and asked Jacques what he wanted. He said a Mimosa would be nice. I poured two, one for each of us.

While we were drinking our drinks, John asked Jacques to make up the gratuity envelopes for the staff. John always had an envelope made for each of the staff that had provided service to us. He told Jacques he would like them before dinner so he could get them ready for tomorrow morning.

Jacques finished his Mimosa. He excused himself, telling us that he would go take care of the envelopes and return with them as quickly as he could.

John walked him to the door, and they stopped for a minute. John was speaking to him in tones so low I couldn't hear what he was saying. I saw Jacques nod his head repeatedly before leaving.

John returned to me and asked if I would like to go shopping and out to lunch before the storm rolled in. I told him I would and we got dressed. As we dressed, I called the front desk and asked them to have the car waiting for us.

When we got downstairs, Jacques was in the lobby, and took John by the arm and pulled him to one side. They spoke in hushed whispers for a moment and John nodded his head, before returning to me. I asked what was going on, and John told me he was arranging for us to have a nice dinner in the suite tonight. I asked if it would be just us at dinner, and he smiled and said, "Yes, tonight is your night." Once again, John had thrilled me with just a few words.

We got into the car, and the driver asked our destination. John told him Les Ambassadeurs, one of the finest jewellery stores in St. Moritz, and my personal favorite. He nodded his head, and we were off. The sky was dark enough that the driver needed his headlights. It wouldn't be long before the storm would arrive. Within 10 minutes, we were at the store and the driver was opening the door for us. The sales clerk had seen the car pull up, and was waiting at the door to open it for us. Although the car had no markings, everyone in St. Moritz recognized the Badrutt's Rolls Royce.

The clerk showed us to a private viewing room. Once seated, she poured the Champagne. The manager came in and introduced herself, telling us her name was Alina and it was a pleasure to have us in her shop. She asked if she could advise us on a purchase, or would we prefer she called the owner to assist us. John told her he was sure her knowledge would be more than sufficient for our needs. She asked what specifically we were looking for, and John told her he wanted a nice necklace and matching bracelet for me. She asked me if I had any special preferences, and I told her I did not, that I would appreciate it if she would make suggestions for me.

After a few more minutes of conversation, she excused herself, telling us she would be right back with several pieces that I might like. In her absence, we sipped our Champagne.

When she returned, she locked the door behind her and sat down with several jewellery presentation folders. She placed them in front of us and slowly opened them.

I was nearly speechless, before me were the most beautiful pieces of jewellery I had ever seen. Each folder contained one gold necklace and one gold bracelet. The one on the left was of an oval link design, and the other a square link design. She brought out her la loupe, a type of magnifying glass and showed us that each individual link had been hand engraved with a beautiful repeating pattern. The engraving caused dramatic light reflection. I asked which she recommended, and she said they were both magnificent.

Recognizing that I was obviously gay, she pointed out that the square link design was very masculine, while the oval was softer and gentler. John laughed at the description of the oval one, saying it was very much like me. We all laughed and she asked if I wanted to try it on. I told her yes, and in a flash the necklace and bracelet were both on me. She held a beautiful viewing mirror for me to see how it looked. I was in love with them. I asked John what he thought, and he agreed they suited me well. Alina smiled, and took the presentation folder, moved it in front of John, and opened a small flap on the back cover.The price of the two pieces was on a small card, only John could see.

John nodded his head and retrieved his wallet from his overcoat pocket. He took his Am Ex Centurion card and slipped it in with the price card. Alina asked if I wanted to wear it, take it with me, or have it shipped to our home. I explained I wasn't dressed to wear it, so we should probably take it with us. John laughed, and said that there was no reason not to wear them. Alina agreed, saying that everything when well with gold, even nakedness. With that comment, she left with the presentation folder.

I thanked John for his special gift, and reminded him that he didn't have to buy me things, that his love was more than enough. He smiled and told me that sometimes love is speechless, and that is when gold speaks eloquently.

Alina returned with the presentation folder, and placed it in front of John. He opened it and took his credit card, then signed the voucher.

Alina gave me a small leather traveling case to carry the jewellery in on the trip home. She also provided a smart leather and black velvet lined case to store it in at home. She asked John who his insurance agent was, so she could have the pieces added to his jewellery insurance policy. He gave her the insurance agent's information. She again told me how good the gold looked on me. She thanked us for our patronage of her store and guided us to the exit.

The driver was waiting and we got into the car. The storm had rolled in, and it was starting to snow when we arrived at the hotel. John asked if I was hungry, and I told him I was, but it was already late and I didn't want to ruin dinner by eating a meal now. He nodded, and suggested that we go to La Grand Hall, and have high tea. I knew he hated high tea, but he was going to do it for me. Once seated, the serving cart arrived with all the pastries and sandwiches. I took a cucumber sandwich, and a couple of sconces. John decided on a couple of smoked salmon sandwiches. As we ordered, a server brought my tea to the table. Only one cup appeared on the table, as the server recognised John and brought him bourbon on the rocks.

We finished our sandwiches while talking about our time together on this trip. I commented on how wonderful this adventure had been, and how much I enjoyed spending time with him. John told me he felt revitalized, and could now return to the world of business. I told him I was looking forward to getting back to Aix, to begin decorating the house for the coming Christmas holiday. I asked where he wanted us to go for the holiday, and to my shock he told me, he wanted to stay at home in Aix. In all our years together, we had always gone to some sun-drenched island for Christmas. I instantly thought about all the things I had to do at home, in the few weeks remaining before Christmas. This would be John's first visit to my home and I wanted everything perfect.

As we approached the door to the suite, the smell of roses scented the air. As we entered, I saw that the dining table was gone, and two massage tables in its place. I asked John what was going on and he said, "You wanted a surprise, now ask no questions." His wicked smile told me this would be a memorable last night in St. Moritz.

As we turned to the living room area, I was overwhelmed to see the largest arrangement of red roses I had ever seen in my life. It filled the fireplace mantle from end to end. In the center of the arrangement was a single yellow rose. John took me by the shoulders and pulled me to him, passionately kissing me as the fire crackled in front of us. When he broke the kiss, I moved to the flowers, and saw a small silver edged card amongst the roses. I took it and read it. On it, "The red roses signify my undying love for you, and the single yellow rose, my joy at knowing you are mine." was neatly scribed in French script.

In seconds, I was in tears, and John was holding me tightly to him. All I could say to him was, "Je t'aime." He responded with, "Mon amour" as he held me tightly until I regained my composure. He led me to the settee and we sat down. He opened the chilled bottle of Champagne, which was on the table, and poured for both of us. We raised our glasses, and toasted our love.

He asked if I wanted him to order dinner, and I told him I wasn't hungry, for food that is. He smiled and asked me to join him in the Jacuzzi tub. I headed for the bathroom, and I heard him talking on the telephone to the front desk. He joined me moments later, and as the tub filled, he turned on the air jets. The pulsing of the warm water on my body caused me an immediate erection, which he noticed. I slipped down slightly in the tub, and stretched my leg out straight, which allowed me to tickle his bollocks with my toes.

I started to slide over to him, so I could provide any services he might require, but he told me not to. He said the evening's plans were in motion and I needed to let them run their course. Moments later, two masseurs entered the bathroom dressed in wine colored posing pouches. I couldn't help but notice how handsome they were, then I realised they were twins. Their muscles rippled, and their pouches strained, attempting to contain their packages.

They each grabbed a towel, and asked us to step out of the tub. We both complied. Soon bundled in towels we were heading to the massage tables, which had soft pads on them, covered with white Egyptian cotton sheets. A small face pillow lay at one end of each table. Aromatherapy candles were burning, and their scent was mixing with the scent of the roses. Suite Bergamasque by DeBussy was playing softly in the background, intensifying the romantic ambience already permeating the room. I felt like my erection was going to rupture if it didn't get some relief.

One of the masseurs asked us to lie face down on the tables, and helped us to position ourselves for comfort. A second linen sheet then covered us. Each table had its own rock hot pot, and I was so pleased to see that the massage would include hot rock therapy.

The masseurs worked on us for over 90 minutes, and when they finished, I felt completely revitalized. One of them asked John if we wanted the traditional "happy ending" with the massage and he told them no, we were saving our semen for each other. They helped us up from the table and wrapped us in our towels.

John and I headed to the bathroom for a warm shower. When we returned from the shower, wrapped in our warm robes, the masseurs had already left.

We retired to the bedroom, and slid under the sheets and duvets. John spooned up behind me, and I automatically raised my leg to allow him to penetrate me. He rubbed his manhood against my love hole, and I could feel that he was already oozing a copious amount of juice. He didn't need any additional lubricant. Once he fully penetrated me, he began to nibble and chew on my earlobe, and took my small pénis in his hand and began to stroke me.

His lovemaking was soft and tender, which was unusual for him. Tonight, I felt that he was actually making love to me, not just alpha male dominating me. I reached for a small towel on the nightstand, slipping it under my pénis, so that I wouldn't shoot my load on the sheets. His thrusting became more rapid, and his breathing more labored. I knew he was approaching his climax, and was surprised it was happening so soon. John usually lasted quite a while. John stopped stroking me, and before I knew it, he was unloading into me, his hot seed spraying my insides. I love the feeling of his semen shooting in me.

Once done, he rolled me onto my back and passionately kissed me. His hot lips locked with mine and his hard tongue found its way into my mouth. From there, he moved to my nipples and worked them into a frenzied state of excitement. Next, it was on to my navel. His tongue drilled it deeply. He continued onward to my phallus, which he slurped into his mouth in a single movement. He worked the head and the shaft until I was quivering.

I finally was able to take no more, and began shooting into his mouth. I grabbed him behind the head and held him tight while my seed filled his mouth. It had been a very long time since I had experienced an orgasm of such intensity. Once I was finished, I looked over at John in time to see him swallow all of the semen I had just unloaded. I was shocked to see him swallow. He was obviously demonstrating his love for me.

He moved back up to my mouth and kissed me, allowing some of my semen to pass from his mouth to mine. Our tongues intertwined and we tongue dueled for a moment or two. John rolled over on his back, and gently stroked my arm with the back of his hand. I rolled over to him, putting my head on his chest. I could hear and feel the rhythmic beating of his heart.

As I lay there on his chest, he twirled my hair between his fingers.

He finally spoke, and began to tell me about his business, his hopes and dreams. He was showing me a side of him that he rarely showed anyone. I decided not to interrupt him with questions or comments, preferring to let him talk. After he had spoken for a while, he looked at me and asked how long we had been together. I replied that in January it would be 23 years. He asked if I was still happy to be with him after all this time. I assured him my love for him had never dwindled; in fact, it had grown as I learned more about him. I wasn't sure what direction this conversation would take, as we had never had an after sex conversation like this ever before.

John got quiet, and I assumed he was gathering his thoughts before continuing our talk. When the pause became too long, I looked up at him and saw that he had fallen asleep while holding me.

I so badly wanted to scream and shout and to wake him up to find out what it was that he was trying to say to me. I knew better. John was one of those men who had to sleep after sex.

I got quietly up from under his arm, and put my robe on. I went out to the living area and found the Champagne still cold. I poured myself a glass, and walked to the balcony doors. The storm had passed, and the sky was crystal clear and jet-black. The light of the quarter moon reflected on both the snow on the ground and the still glass-like surface of the lake.

Looking out over the lake, I realised that I was just going to have to wait for tomorrow to find out exactly what John was talking about. I looked at my wine glass and it was empty, so I turned back to the living area to refill it.

Chapter 19

After two more glasses of Champagne, I went back to bed. John was sleeping and I slid under the covers and snuggled next to him. He readjusted his position, but didn't wake.

I woke a short time later to the sensation of John nibbling and sucking on my ear. He would bite the lobe, and then drill my ear canal with his tongue. I knew he was already ready for round two. I let him play with my ear for a couple of minutes, and then I reached back and took his hardness in my hand. When I gripped him, he rolled onto his back and told me to ride him. I knelt over him, and allowed his manhood to connect with my love tunnel.

I had more than enough of his juice in me, and when I pushed down, I engulfed his pole. I slid all the way down, feeling his bollocks pressing against my cheeks. He didn't move, preferring to wait for me to begin the ride.

I pulled up slowly while squeezing my sphincter tightly, providing maximum tightness to his phallus. Once at the top, I did a slow downward slide, while relaxing my sphincter. I started the repetitive up and down cycle, keeping a slow and steady speed. I was waiting for John to begin thrusting into me before I sped up the cycle.

He let me ride him for nearly 30 minutes before I felt the first thrust from him. I immediately began increasing my riding speed. Soon, I had him bucking under me while I rode him. In short order, he was grunting and moaning. I felt a particularly forceful push from him, and then he grabbed my hips and pulled me down onto him. I felt him swell and pulse, and without stopping, he began unloading his seed into me. When he was finished, he slowly stopped thrusting, allowing me to sit on him.

We didn't speak, preferring instead to bask in the afterglow of our lovemaking. When he finally pulled himself out of me, I rolled off him and lay next to him on my back.

He spoke first, asking me if I was looking forward to going home. I told him I always looked forward to going home, just not, his continuing on to America. I also told him I understood that our arrangement was necessary. There was no way for me to fit into his world of straight men and high finance, since I was too gay and flamboyant for his business associates.

He asked me if I could ever leave France permanently, and I told him I didn't think so. Then he said, "Would you leave if I asked you to?" I wondered what was going on with these questions, and said to him, "France has been my home for my entire life, and my family has lived in Aix since the 15th century. I love my home, but I love you more. If you insist that I leave France, I will, but only because of my love for you."

He stared into my face, seeing the tears welling up. He asked, "You really love me that much?" I nodded my head yes.

After a minute of awkward silence, I asked him why he would want me to leave France. He told me he was thinking about stepping down as CEO of his company and becoming the Chairman of the Board. Effectively, he would retire. He said he was thinking of many places we could retire to, and he needed to know if I would go with him. I told him I would go with him anywhere he chose.

He told me not to worry about it, that it was just a thought and he wanted my opinion. I told him retirement was an excellent idea that would allow us to make up for some of the time we had been apart because of his business.

He then changed topics, telling me he had arranged for us to check out early so we could make the train to Chur by 7am. I looked at the clock, and it was already 4am, so I decided to get up and start the day. I asked John why he chose such an early train, when our flight from

Zurich left in late afternoon. He looked at me and said, "We're taking the train all the way home." I was shocked. He never liked the train, he felt it was too slow, and the train station in Paris was not convenient to the airport. He said not to worry everything was taken care of.

I called room service to bring up café for us. I thought we would need it for such an early start.

I got up from the bed, and made my way to the shower. As the hot water ran over me, I could feel John's semen leaking from me. I was shampooing my hair when John stepped into the shower. He came up behind me, and I felt his erection against the back of my leg. Without opening my eyes, I asked him why he was so overly excited this morning. He usually took an hour or more to recover and be ready to begin lovemaking again. He told me I excited him and his manhood wanted more of me.

I knew I still had enough of his semen in me that I didn't need any additional lubricant, so I bent over putting my head under the water. While the water was rinsing the shampoo from my hair, John penetrated me in a single forceful thrust. He grunted as his bollocks slapped against me. He grabbed my shoulders, and began rough riding me. He slammed into me repeatedly, striking my prostate with each thrust. Soon, my pénis was rock hard and leaking. Johns grunting turned into animalistic noises, and his thrusting became faster and rougher.

I put my hand on the top of my head so it wouldn't slam into the shower wall as he pounded me. I felt his hands slide down to my hips and pull me back on to him. He stopped thrusting and I felt his hot sperm flying into me. When he finished and pulled out, semen ran down my bollocks and the backs of my legs.

He helped me to a standing position, and I asked him if he was done, or should I wait on showering in case he wanted round four. He laughed and told me he was finished for the moment.

I finished my shower, and while I dried off, John got in. While he was shampooing his hair, I saw his phallus hardening again. I wondered what was going on; I thought that maybe he had taken Viagra. When he stepped out of the shower I asked him about taking Viagra, and he told me he had not. It seemed that with this being our last day together, his pénis was trying to wear itself out. I asked if he wanted assistance with the hardness, and he told me no, the head was much too sensitive for any more stimulation at that moment.

As we both dressed, a soft knock at the door announced the arrival of the café cart.

Jacques brought the cart in, set up, and served us. John asked him to join us. After pouring himself a cup of café, he told John that our travel plans guaranteed and the reservations made. He handed John a leather pouch with the hotel's crest on it and our names imprinted on it. John took the pouch and went to the bedroom to put it in his suit jacket pocket.

Jacques told me the train was leaving St. Moritz at 10am, and that the car would pick us up at 9am. He was sending our luggage ahead to the station, as soon as the staff had it packed.

John came out of the bedroom dressed in his traveling clothes, and suggested I get dressed too. He asked Jacques to call the staff to come in and pack our luggage. As I went to change, I heard Jacques on the telephone ordering the staff to our suite.

When I came out from the bedroom, the chambermaids were waiting to get our packing done. Jacques was again on the telephone arranging something John asked for. With so much activity going on, I decided I needed to help by sitting down and having a Mimosa.

The chambermaids packed the luggage in record time, and the bellman arrived with his cart to take it downstairs. The delivery van was waiting to take it to the train station.

It was 7o'clock when John came over and took my hand. He said we had business downstairs to take care of. Jacques escorted us to the lobby.

A small group of staff assembled in the library, and we joined them. The hotel general manager attended with his staff. John took a moment to thank them for their excellent service during our stay. He assured them that they were the reason we returned repeatedly to Badrutts. He told them that service of this caliber was unmatched anywhere else in the world. Then he told them that as a thank you Jacques had an envelope for each of them. He then handed the 27 envelopes to Jacques. As the staff left the room, they stopped and shook our hands and John and I again thanked them for their service. On the way out the door, they picked up their envelopes from Jacques.

When everyone was gone, the general manager came over. He thanked us for staying at Badrutt's, and invited us to return soon. John thanked him as he made his way out the door. Jacques was the only one remaining in the room with us, and John put out his hand to shake Jacques. John told him that his drive for excellence was outstanding and we appreciated all his attention to the details, which made our stay so enjoyable. John then reached into his jacket, pulled out Jacques envelope, and handed it to him. He took it and discretely put it into his own pocket. Once again, with thanks all around, we headed out the door.

When we stepped into the lobby, we saw the car just pulling up at the doors. The general manager walked us to the door and out to the car. He thanked us again for staying with him. John nodded and we got into the car.

There was no morning traffic, so the ride to the station was short. When we arrived, the driver held the door for us as we got out. Once out, John thanked him for all the driving and waiting that he had done with us. The driver said it was his pleasure to provide service to us. John reached into his pants pocket and produced two five hundred dollar bills, which he pressed into the driver's hand. We turned and made our way up the stairs to the station.

The chief porter saw us approaching the train, and came over to us. He introduced himself and showed us to our cabin. It was small but nice, and Badrutt's had arranged a continental breakfast for us. The chief porter let himself out, and we sat down. John and I both picked up our café and sipped on the hot liquid.

John and I sat talking, and soon a service boy knocked on the door. He asked if he could remove the breakfast plates, as we would be departing the station in a few minutes. John told him to go head. The boy quickly cleared all the dishes and left.

I asked John how much money he had put in the envelopes for the staff, and he told me that they had each received one thousand dollars in their envelope. I asked him about Jacques, and he told me Jacques had received five thousand dollars. He said Jacques was special, because he could meet our needs even before we knew they were needs. He also reminded me that a special gratuity was in order for my special early morning shower sex, which he had so excellently provided.

I was going to respond, but we felt the train jerk, and we were pulling out of the station. The service boy returned with several heavy fur blankets for us, in the event we got cold during the trip to Chur. He told us the travel time would be approximately two hours.

After he left, we turned our seats to face the window, and watched as the train pulled away from the station. With the armrest up, the chairs became a small loveseat. Soon we were traveling through the Swiss countryside.

John moved closer to me, until his leg pressed against mine. I dropped my hand to his lap, and found that he was fully erect, straining the zipper of his pants. I gently massaged him for a couple of minutes before unzipping him and releasing his manhood. I again thought it was unusual for him to have so many erections in such a short period.

I leaned over his lap to service him, but he pulled my head up and kissed me. He then told me to get out of my clothes and kneel on the loveseat cushions. I did as he directed, draping myself over the back of the loveseat. I had a beautiful view out the window, with the snow falling and the countryside rolling past.

I felt John behind me, and then he applied lube to me. He wasted no time in sliding his fingers into me to spread the lubricant around. In a matter of moments, I felt his phallus rubbing up and down my cleft. He slapped my bum, and caused me to take a sharp breath in. as I did; he slid his entire maleness into me in one thrust, and striking my prostate and making me tingle. He held still for several minutes, perhaps enjoying the warmth of my tunnel, before He began his usual thrusting. It was interesting to have his hardness in me while I looked out at the scenery. I also discovered that I could see his reflection in the window while he pounded me.

While we were enjoying our playtime, there was a knock at the door. John withdrew from me, and told me to stay where I was. I looked over my shoulder, and saw the young service boy standing in the door. John invited him in and told him to strip. Apparently, John had arranged this little "party" when we boarded the train. The boy quickly shed his clothes, and stood staring at me. He was hard; his pénis long and thin, with a foreskin that completely covered the head. John told me the boy was a gay virgin, and wanted to try gay sex. He asked if I would allow the boy to mount me. I told him of course I would, and John got a condom out of his jacket, which was hanging on the back of the door.

He took the boy's sausage in his hand and skinned the foreskin back. He put the condom over the head and rolled it all the way down to the base of the shaft. He then pulled the foreskin back up, and finished unrolling the condom.

He led the boy to me, and positioned him so he could mount me. The boy timidly pushed the head against me, and John told him to push harder. The boy did, and entered me. I tightened my sphincter, wanting to provide as much stimulation as possible. Once he was all the way in, John told him to start thrusting.

While the boy started thrusting, John got behind him and lubricated his fingers. When the boy pulled back, John slipped a finger into him. The boy froze, and gasped. He told John it hurt, and John told him that it wouldn't hurt for long. The boy resumed his thrusting, and soon John had him completely loosened up. John then took up a position behind the boy and told him to thrust all the way into me and hold it there. The boy did, and when he stopped, John penetrated him. The boy howled, but John just continued pushing until he was balls deep in the boy. He waited a minute for the boy to adjust to having a pénis in him, and then began thrusting.

On the second or third thrust, the boy gasped and unloaded his sperm. I could feel the warmth of it inside his condom. John continued thrusting until he reached his orgasm and poured his semen into the boy. While his hot semen filled him, the boy reached a second climax and ejaculated again into the condom. This second climax combined with my own manual stimulation pushed me over the top and I unloaded against the back of the loveseat.

When they were finished, John withdrew from the boy, and the boy withdrew from me. John moved up to my face and allowed me to clean his phallus. His sperm had run down his shaft and on to his bollocks. Once I had him clean, I turned around and sat on the loveseat. I pulled the boy to me and removed his condom, which was nearly a quarter of the way full. I then cleaned him up.

John congratulated him on losing his gay virginity, and asked if he would have gay sex again. The boy smiled and nodded his head yes, while he put his uniform back on. He thanked us, and let himself out of the cabin. As he went out the door, I saw him reach back and rub his sore, no longer virgin boyhole.

I asked John what that was all about, and he told me simply, that the boy and approached him when we boarded the train. Apparently, someone at Badrutt's Palace had told him that we were always on the look-out for good-looking men to join us in a ménage à trois. He wanted to try sex with men and thought this might be his opportunity. John then told me it had been awhile since he had taken a young man's virginity and saw no reason not to.

I went into the bathroom and cleaned myself up, and got dressed. John was dressed when I came out of the bathroom; I went over and cleaned my semen from the back of the loveseat. When I was done, the cabin looked as if nothing had happened.

John suggested we go to the club car and get a drink. I was all for it.

Chapter 20

Once seated in the club car, John ordered drinks for both of us, Bourbon for himself and a split of Champagne for me. We moved to a table by a window and sat down. I gazed out the window, watching the beautiful countryside roll by. It was starting to snow more heavily than when we started out from St. Moritz. The trip to Chur from St. Moritz was only two hours, so we had less than 30 minutes to our first train change. From Chur we would transfer to the Zurich train, and then on to Paris, where John would catch his flight to Los Angeles.

When conversation seemed appropriate, I asked John if he had arranged any other sexual encounters for us on the way to Paris. He told me he liked the idea of quickie sex on each leg of the journey. I couldn't help but smile, my alpha male, always ready to breed with someone.

As we pulled into the station at Chur, the chief porter knocked on our door and offered to escort us to our next train. We slipped into our coats, and followed him to the back of the train. There was a VIP exit, which would allow us to change trains without being caught in the crowd.

We boarded the train for Zurich, and since the ride was only an hour and one half, we were seated in the first class lounge. There was no cabin car attached to this train. When we were seated, the bar steward brought us Bourbon and Champagne. The train did have restaurant service, but the quality of the food is so poor that we passed on lunch. John told me he had talked with Jacques at the hotel, and asked him to get a catered picnic lunch put on board the train in Zurich for us.

I couldn't help but think that John was not going to be able to arrange any quickie sex on this train. We had no cabin, and even if we had a fur blanket, it was broad daylight and it would be obvious what we were doing.

Time would also be an issue, as the trip was only 90 minutes.

When John finished his drink, he took me by the hand and led me towards the back of the train. When we reached the baggage car, he knocked, and the door was opened by a very cute young man.

Once inside, John told me to get out of my clothes while he and the young man undressed. John usually introduced me to any men he intended to have sex with, but this was obviously not going to happen. Once I was naked, John bent me over a large padded shipping crate. He got his tube of lubricant and slicked me up. He didn't bother with any of the niceties; this was going to be strictly a quick rough ride.

As he moved up behind me, I felt him rubbing his head against my love hole. With a quick couple of swipes to spread the lubricant around, he shoved himself balls deep into me, making me gasp. Once in me, he motioned to the young man to step up in front of me. He looked to be 19 or 20 years-old, with a firm slender body, and a nice 7 inch pénis. He was also circumcised, which is unusual for a European man. I asked about the circumcision, and he told me he had caught his foreskin in the zipper of his pants when he was a child, developed an infection, and circumcision was the only choice to solve the problem. I nodded my head in understanding. I took his hardness in my hand, and proceeded to pull him towards me, licking the tip, and sliding my tongue up his hard shaft.

A couple trips of my tongue up and down his pole, and he was leaking copious amounts of juice. I repeatedly licked the juice from the tip before engulfing the entire head into my mouth. Since he had no foreskin, I locked my lip just behind the head and started a light sucking motion. As he began grunting, I increased the pressure and engulfed the entire shaft into my mouth. I let him push himself balls deep, and when his bollocks slapped my chin he erupted in my mouth, shooting hot sperm deeply into my throat. After several powerful shots, I pulled back so he would shoot across my tongue and fill my mouth so I could get a good taste of his juice. He remained hard, and I allowed him to stay in my mouth.

I was disappointed that once again I had ended up with a premature ejaculator. I gave his phallus a sperm bath before swallowing all of his seed. When he still made no move to pull out, I began to fellate him again. This time, I used long slow strokes, from tip to base in an attempt to prevent a second premature ejaculation. The technique worked, and he worked himself in and out of my mouth with deliberate slowness. I felt John speeding up, and then heard him give out a quiet moan. I began squeezing my sphincter as hard as possible, and I felt him pulse and expand inside me. He slammed me with a couple of rapid fire thrusts, and then buried himself deeply in me while he filled me with his semen.

When he finished, he pulled out and handed me a condom to put on our young friend. When the boy saw it, he pulled himself from my mouth, and waited patiently for me to get it on him. When I had the condom in place, he and John switched places.

John wasted no time in stuffing his pénis into my mouth, and he motioned for the young man to mount me. The boy took his time, and gently penetrated me before beginning his thrusting action. He made sure to hit my prostate with each inward thrust, providing me a tingle each time. I was now leaking, and John reached under me and started to stroke me using my juice to slick me up. John kept pace with the boy, and soon the boy and I were both unloading. I could feel the hot sperm in the condom in me, and my own seed was spraying out over John's hand, cascading onto the padding on the shipping crate. When we were finished, the boy pulled out of me, leaving me with an empty feeling. He removed his condom and chucked it into the trash receptacle near the door.

John handed me a small towel to clean up with and then we dressed. Without a word, John took me by the hand and escorted me out the door.

We went back to the club car, and took our previous seats. The bar steward brought us new drinks, and we sat sipping them. I told John I had doubts about his being able to arrange a sexual encounter on this short leg of the trip, and he told me I should never doubt him.

The porter came around and let us know that the train would be pulling into Zurich in approximately 15 minutes, and he would be back to escort us to the next train.

Once he had left the table, I asked John why he didn't introduce me to the boy in the baggage car. He told me that sometimes it was best for a quickie encounter to be completely anonymous. That way I could fantasize anything I wanted to about the boy. He also reminded me to never under estimate his ability to arrange a quick sex encounter anywhere. I had to admit that I didn't think he would be able to make it happen on such a short trip and one without cabins.

As we pulled into Zurich, the porter returned and showed us to the VIP exit, leading us to platform 15 where the TVG (high speed train) 9222was waiting. Having made this trip more than a few times, I knew that the TGV to Paris left from platform 9, TGV 9210. I asked the porter about the mix-up, and he showed me the boarding passes for TGV 9222. I looked at John and he smiled and told me not to worry about it. I asked the porter where the train went, and he told me Dijon Ville. Dijon Ville is nowhere near the route to Paris. In fact, it is just north of Lyon which is the train line to Aix-en-Provence and Marseilles. I was seriously confused, and John seemed to find it funny. I asked the porter where the train's final destination was, and he told me Aix-en-Provence.

I asked John why he was going so far out of his way, and he told me he thought he would try flying to L.A. from Marseilles, as they have a flight that is only 14 hours, with a quick stop in London.

He told me he wanted to have one day with me in Aix. He had never seen my city home, and had only seen pictures of my ancestral home, and wanted to see both in person. I assured him that my homes were nowhere near as fancy as his California home and condo.

We settled in to the first class seating area, and the bar steward instantly appeared. He asked our drink preference, and John told him he wanted Bourbon, and I told him that I would have a Cosmopolitan. John reminded me that I had been drinking Champagne all day, and did I really want to mix Champagne and distilled spirits. I thought about it, and decided that if John was going home with me, the last thing I wanted to do was get drunk on a train. I corrected my order to a Mimosa, and the steward left to get our drinks.

I asked John about his sudden interest in my homes, and he laughed and told me it was time for him to learn more about Aix-en-Provence and France in general, since I had traveled the world with him and learned about the places he liked.

Our drinks arrived, and with them, our picnic lunch. It was a large basket, and it had the Badrutt's crest on the top. The steward asked if he should unpack it for us or did we wish to do it ourselves. John told him we would, and took the basket from him. We were sitting at a table for four, and had plenty of space to setup our basket.

When he opened it, John retrieved the china plates, and the silver flatware, then the linen napkins and the glassware. I set the table for us, as John brought out the food.

The hotel restaurant had provided an appetizer of, Pear, Roquefort and Rosemary tart. Next was the Creamy Chicken and Garlic Picnic Pasties, a salad of fresh fig and Feta cheese with walnuts, Marianne Baguette, and an apricot tart for desert. These were certainly not the kinds of foods that John would order in a restaurant. He said he told the hotel to provide us with a typical Provence picnic.

After lunch, we returned to the first class car, and took our previous seats. We had a beautiful view out the bubble windows. The hotel had made our reservation for seats on the east side of the train, as the sun would be setting during this leg of the journey, and they didn't want us squinting to see the countryside.

The trip to Dijon Ville would only take two and one-half hours, as the train's average speed was over 200 mph. I was wondering how John would pull off another sexual encounter, since we were already down to one and one-half hours travel time.

A few moments later, the porter came over to our table and told John he had an international call in the chief porter's office. John thanked him and invited me to join him. We made our way to the office, and John knocked on the door. When the door opened, we were invited in. The office was small, but well appointed. There was a good sized desk, a leather sofa, and a recliner lounge chair. John and the porter were talking like they were old friends, when John began to remove his clothes. I knew this was the encounter for this leg of the trip and began undressing myself. The chief porter waited until we were both naked, before stripping off his own clothes. He then went over and locked the office door.

When he stepped out from behind his desk, I looked him over. He was in his mid to upper fifties, pudgy, and definitely out of shape. His abdomen hung down to his pubic hair, nearly covering his very small pénis. I couldn't figure out why John would select such a person to join us.

The porter then came over to me, and looked me over. He commented on my lack of foreskin, pulling his own out several inches from the shrunken head. He had an unpleasant, unwashed smell that I found offensive. He began stroking himself, and as he began to harden, I saw why John had invited him to join us. He was half hard and already 8 inches. By the time he finished erecting, he was very close to 11 inches. Fortunately, he was about the same width as John, which meant he wouldn't stretch me to the point of pain.

John told me to get in position on the sofa, and I climbed up and kneeled on the seat cushions. I leaned against the back, and waited to see who would mount me first. I heard John tell the porter to put on a condom, and then I knew the porter would be first. John came up behind me, and I felt cold lubricant being rubbed into my manhole, followed by three of John's fingers. He obviously felt a rudimentary stretching was in order. He quickly withdrew, and told the porter to mount me.

The porter did as instructed and single push penetrated me. There wasn't any pain until he hit my prostate and continued pushing the rest of his 11 inches in. I felt his phallus slide past my prostate and continue up my colon. He finally got himself balls deep, and paused to catch his breath. While the porter was penetrating me, John came around to the front of me and stuck his member into my mouth. I immediately began fellating him.

I am not sure why, but I wasn't enjoying the sex at all. John seemed distracted, and the porter was only interested in his own satisfaction. I was hoping that they would both prematurely ejaculate and get it over with.

The porter dumped his load after about 3 minutes, and instantly pulled out of me. I was grateful. John lasted only a few minutes more, and unloaded. This time, his ejaculation wasn't powerfully shot, it was weak and dribbling. I still took all he had and swallowed. He withdrew, and we both got dressed. The chief porter invited us back to see him anytime we were on his train. My parting thought was, "Not if yours was the last pénis on the planet."

When we got back to our seats, John apologized for his poor performance. I told him that with all the ejaculating he had done today, I was surprised he could still get a hard-on this late in the day. He then asked about the porter, and by the look on his face I knew, that he knew, I wasn't happy with the man.

I told him that just because a man has a lengthy organ, doesn't mean he knows how to use it or can interact socially with those he would like to use it on. I told John quite bluntly that the man was a clod and a swine, and that I would never allow him to touch me again. John explained that he had been told about the man's unusual size, and thought I might like to try my talents out on him. He said he had no idea that the man was a pig. I told him to forget it, that he could make it up to me at Pellegrin and Fils when we got to Aix. The bar steward announced the bar was closed, as we were only 15 minutes from Dijon.

John and I decided we would get a crêpe or croissant in the train station while waiting on our connection to Aix, and then eat dinner in Aix. We would be leaving Dijon around 7pm, and arriving in Aix at 1030pm. A late bistro supper would be very nice.

Our one hour train change in Dijon was uneventful, and when we boarded the train to Aix, it was already dark. We got comfortable in our lounge chairs, and the porter brought out furry blankets for all the first class passengers. He explained that they were working on the heating system and that as soon as the train departed the station the climate control system would engage, turning on the heat. We cuddled up under the blankets, and in a couple of minutes the train was leaving the station.

I turned to speak to John, and found that he had slumped over onto my shoulder and was asleep. I called the porter, and he brought us pillows, and helped me adjust John's seat so it was reclining back. He then helped me recline mine, and I was then able to move John's head to my chest. As he lay sleeping, I couldn't help but wonder why John was doing these things.

By nature he is a man of habit, and rarely changed his routines. I couldn't find a logical reason for him to be making this side trip to Aix. With my mind racing in many directions, I stared out the bubble windows into the night.

Chapter 21

When I awoke, it took me a minute to remember I was on the train home. I pulled my arm out from under the blanket, and looked at my watch. It was almost 9pm. I had slept almost two hours. The porter must have seen that I was awake, and he came over to see if I needed anything. John lay comfortably on his side, which allowed the porter to help me sit my recliner up. I took a few minutes to resettle myself, and then realized I needed the bathroom. As if by magic, the porter appeared and helped me to my feet. He directed me to the "water closet" (restroom). On the way, I noticed that the first class seating area had only a dozen people. John and I sat at the very front, so we had an unobstructed view. The next nearest passengers to us were about eight rows behind us. We had a proper first class cabin in terms of area. After relieving myself, I returned to my seat to see that the pillows fluffed, and a clean blanket had replaced the one I slept in.

Once I resettled myself, the porter arrived with café au lait for me. I smelled wonderful, and the warmth helped to take the chill off the evening air. The porter asked if I was cold, and when I told him yes, he adjusted the heating vents.

I looked over at John, and he continued to sleep. I thought to myself that all the sex of the day had caught up to him and he had worn himself out. I sat drinking my café, as John started to move around. He finally turned over so that he was facing me. I thought about waking him up, so he would be able sleep when we got home, but changed my mind.

I thought to myself that John's plan for sex on each leg of the journey home looked like it wasn't going to happen. We were only an hour from Aix, and there didn't seem to be any real possibility of it happening. I bend down over John and couldn't resist the opportunity to show him he was wrong. I whispered, "No sex on the last leg John, I think your plan failed." I chuckled quietly to myself. I sat there gloating for a minute before I felt John's hand reach out for mine and pull it under his blanket. He directed me to his lap, where his manhood was fully erect and ready for action. He wrapped my hand around his phallus, and I knew he wanted me to masturbate him.

I began the process by playing with his foreskin, and rubbing the head gently with my fingers. He stretched and repositioned himself to provide me with better access to his throbbing organ. I massaged his bollocks and worked his shaft, thinking to myself that with only a short nap this man was rock hard and ready.

The porter came by while I was playing with John, and he knew immediately what was happening. He turned down our night-lights, and excused himself, telling us he would not return until we called for him.

Once the porter was out of earshot, John pulled his blanket down, revealing his stiff rod. With his foreskin pulled tightly back, I could see that the head was deep red and pulsing. I leaned over and took it in my mouth, savoring the taste of the juices leaking from him. I finally took his shaft all the way into my throat and when my nose hit his pubes, I was able to lick his balls at the same time. I was really getting into the oral work, when he pulled me off him. In a low voice, he told me to recline my chair, slip my pants down to my knees and turn over on my side.

I did as he directed, and quite quickly, I felt his hands spreading my cheeks, and his mushroom head sliding up and down my cleft. I bore down to help open my anus to him, and when I did, he slipped his hardness in. He toyed with me, putting it in only an inch or two then pulling it out. After a few minutes, I was pushing back and begging him to penetrate me fully. He finally decided to, and with a full pull out, he then slammed back in with a single rough stroke. I felt my prostate electrify as his member rubbed against me.

He continued to pummel me until he felt my sphincter squeezing him in anticipation of my impending orgasm. He increased his speed and depth of penetration, and I unloaded on to my blanket. John went a couple more minutes, and then unloaded in me. His powerful jetting had returned as he pumped half dozen squirts deeply into me. We remained in our positions for a little while before John pulled out of me and we were able to rearrange our clothing and put our seats upright once again.

I called for the porter, and explained that my blanket required laundering. He gave me an ear-to-ear smile, and told me it wasn't a problem. He returned a short time later, bringing two cafés au lait and several small hand towels for me. John drank his café while I went to the water closet to clean myself up.

When I returned, John was smiling. He looked at me and said, "Do not underestimate me, if I say sex on each leg of a journey, there will be sex on each leg of the journey." I laughed, and told him I believed him. I sat down next to him and drank my café.

The porter came by and told us we were 15 minutes from Aix. I looked out the window and saw that the snow had long stopped. It rarely snows in Aix. He asked us to collect any belongings we had brought on board and that he would be back to escort us to the VIP exit, when we reached the station. He also told us it was 10°C. I converted it for John and told him the temperature was about 50°F. We both slipped on our coats, but didn't button them up.

We heard the automated sound system announce our arrival in Aix, along with some information for passengers continuing on the Marseilles.

The porter returned a few minutes later, and led us to the VIP exit. John thanked him for his service, and for taking care of the blanket that needed laundering. He put his hand in his pocket, retrieving a one hundred Euro bill, and passed it to the porter when he shook his hand.

As we disembarked, I remembered that I had forgotten to call my neighbor to pick us up. I shouldn't have worried. John had the hotel arrange a limousine to take us home from the TVG station. The driver greeted us by name, and opened the door for us. Once we settled in, the driver got in and began the drive home.

I asked John if he still wanted a late supper and he told me he did. I asked the driver to take us to "Ze Bistro," a small place I frequent. The food is always good, the service impeccable, and the ambience romantic.

When we arrived, the driver aided us in exiting the car, and told us he would be here when we were ready to go home.

As we entered the bistro, one of the owners, Albert, came running over to give me a bear hug and kisses to both cheeks. He asked how the trip was, and then turning to John asked who the handsome man was. I opened my mouth to speak, and found myself speechless. I had never had the opportunity to introduce John to anyone, and I wasn't sure if he wanted to me to introduce him as my partner. A moment of awkward silence ensued, and then John broke it by saying to Albert, that he was my husband. Albert was shocked, and then grabbed John hugging him and giving the mandatory kisses to each cheek.

Albert looked at me and said, "I thought this man was a fantasy of yours, why have we never seen him here?" John spoke up and explained our arrangement to Albert. Albert's response was that he hoped we would see more of him in the future.

Albert showed us to my favorite table, where we could sit and look out over Rue Manuel. We watched the people who were leaving from Théâtre Ateliers' last performance, while waiting for our drinks.

The barman brought us a bottle of Champagne in a wine cooler, and set it up tableside. Albert brought us smoked duck and cheese on pesto toast points. He also brought out the traditional crudités.

As we ate, I finally got up enough nerve to ask John, "Now tell me why you really wanted to come to Aix with me. I know that it has nothing to do with learning about France."

John stared over at me with a most serious look on his face, and said, "I know that you love me beyond measure, and I think I am finally realizing that there are more important things in life than making money. I have amassed a large fortune, and my investments add to it daily. There is no way you and I could spend all the money that I have already put away." He took a sip of his wine and continued. "When I spoke to you earlier about stepping down as CEO of the company, I was trying to see what your reaction would be. As always, you were more concerned about me than you were. Your selflessness in telling me you would leave your beloved France for me was overwhelming. I decided at that moment that love was far more important than money could ever be. "

He took a deep breath, then several sips of his wine before continuing, "At that moment, I felt like my eyes had been opened to how all encompassing your love for me is. All of these emotions and logic have led me to the conclusion that I have done you a grave disservice in not having you with me all the time." At this point, I was holding myself together by a thread, tears welling up in my eyes, and a slight fear as to what he might say next. He reached across the table, took my hand, and held it tightly in his. Then he said the words that would change my life and his forever. "Effective in less than an hour, I will no longer be the CEO of my company. I have retired." I was so hoping that he would say those words, but I was shocked that he had done it.

He continued to hold my hand, while taking several more sips of his wine. With a slight hesitation in his voice, he said, "I know that you love France more than anywhere else on earth. I have never known such an attachment to a place, and have a hard time understanding it." My next thought was that he was going to ask me to leave my home and follow him. I was dreading it, leaving France was the very last thing I wanted to do. The tears finally broke, and ran down my face. He reached over with his free hand, and wiped them away, as he said, "Don't worry mon ami, I will never ask you to leave your home. Instead, I have decided that I would like to make my home here in Aix with you, if you will allow it." There was such a weight lifted from my heart that I couldn't hold the tears back any longer. His free hand went into his jacket pocket, and he brought out a small black velvet box. The crest on the box was Cartier, and as he set it down on the table, he opened it. I glanced inside at the most gorgeous ring I had ever seen. I looked up at him just as he asked, "Will you marry me?"

I was speechless. I never expected to hear those words from John's mouth. He had told me in the beginning of our relationship that he could never publicly acknowledge his love for me. He said he was destined to remain the in closet for the rest of his life. He did tell me however, that if he ever came out of the closet, everyone would know of his love for me.

I told him of course I would marry him, and he told me he would like to be married in Amsterdam on New Year's Day. With that said, he took the ring from the box and slipped it on my finger.

Now fully overwhelmed by the events of the day I lost all my composure and began openly crying at the table. Albert came rushing over to see what the problem was, and when I showed him, the ring he hugged me began crying too. When we regained some level of calmness, Albert asked the musicians to play a waltz.

As the music began, John moved to my side and held out his hand to me. I rose from my chair, and he took me in his arms and passionately kissed me in public, for the very first time. He broke the kiss, and led me to the small dance floor. As we began the dance, the patrons in the restaurant began to applaud us. We danced several turns on the floor, before returning to our table.

Once seated, I asked John what he thought he could do in Aix to occupy his retirement time. He said he expected me to spend many hours acquainting him with Aix. He also told me he wanted me to teach him to speak fluent French. After that, if we got bored, he would buy us a yacht and we could spend our days sailing. Monaco is less than 200 miles away, and makes a great sailing trip. After that, the world is the limit. We can go anywhere we want.

We finished our dinner, and with hugs and kisses all around, we made our exit. The limousine and driver were waiting, and we got in. The driver asked if we wanted to go home and I told him I did.

It was a short ride to my house in the city. I knew that it was nothing compared to what John had left in California, but I loved it and it fit me well.

When we arrived, the driver took us up the circular driveway, and stopped at the front doors. He helped us disembark, and John thanked him and provided a large gratuity.

We moved up to the door, and I slipped my key into the lock. As I unlocked the door, I warned John the house would probably not meet his expectations. City homes in Aix are usually multiple hundreds of years old, and as such, they are small. As we entered, John took in the sights of my home, our home. The foyer was marble with polished walnut accents. The staircase was circular and went gracefully up to the next floor. I tossed my key on the table, and saw the pile of mail the neighbor had collected for me.

I gave John a short tour of the house, explaining that some distant relatives of mine had built it in the 18th century. After I showed him the inside, I took him out back to the garden. There was a large reflecting pond and the landscaping immaculate. We sat by the pool enjoying the coolness of the evening.

John asked why he had never seen any bills for the maintenance and upkeep on the house. I told him that I didn't need his money to keep my own home maintained. He then asked what I did for a living that I could afford this home without his assistance.

I had to laugh, as I told John that people like me don't work. He looked puzzled, and I pressed on with the explanation. I asked if he remembered the painting of the large country home that hung in the foyer. He said he did, that it seemed immense in size. I told him that it wasn't just a painting of a house; it was a painting of my country home. King Louis XI had deeded the land to my family in 1487, in recognition of their support during the long wars with England. Since I inherited the property, I had retained a small handful of people to oversee the grapes and the making of the wine. The property supported me with a large yearly stipend, and it was more than I could spend. Through the years, I had banked any money from the stipend that I didn't use to live on. I then told him I had a wise investment broker in California who had made my money work for me and added nicely to the balances in my accounts.

For the first time ever, John looked surprised. He asked why I had never told him any of this, especially the fact that I had money invested in his company. I explained that since he had never asked about my finances, I didn't see any reason to volunteer the information. He looked like he wanted to continue the conversation, but I cut him off and told him it was time for bed.

We went upstairs to the bedroom, and I stripped out of my stale traveling clothes. I walked to the shower, and invited John to join me. He too stripped and soon we were both in the shower. The hot water felt good on the muscles that had stiffened during the trip. I washed John's back and bottom and he washed mine. After shampooing our hair, we stepped out of the shower onto the warmed tile floor. John had an erection, and I pointed at it and told him I would take care of that as soon as we got into bed. In the bedroom, I got out two fluffy robes similar to the ones Badrutt's had.

I helped John into his, and then put on mine. John noticed the embroidered crest on the robes and asked if it was a family crest. I nodded and told him it was. He remarked that he should have known. From the dressing room, we went into the bedroom and found that the fire was bright and cheery, warming the entire room. In the sitting area, there was a silver service tray with hot chocolate and chocolate croissants.

I invited John to join me at the table and he did. As we sipped our chocolate, he looked around the room, noting some similarities to Badrutt's. John got up and went out the French doors that opened on to a balcony, which provided a breathtaking panoramic view of the surrounding hill and the city. He told me he almost felt like he was back at Badrutt's.

I put my hot chocolate down, and took John's cup from him. I led him to the tuned down bed, which was ready for us.

John suddenly asked who lit the fire, brought up the hot chocolate, and turned down the bed. I told him that my valet had taken care of those chores for us. He was going to say more, but I put my finger to his lips indicating silence. I removed his robe and had him climb into the luxurious bed. I shed my robe and joined him. We snuggled under the duvet, and I felt John's erect phallus poking me. I rolled over on my side, giving John room to spoon up against me. I lifted my leg, and provided him access to my warm and ready love chute. He wasted no time in accepting the opportunity, and slid his manhood deeply into me.

As he began long, slow thrusts of lovemaking, I felt my entire body relax. Suddenly everything seemed so right, it was as if we were destined to live in Aix, in my home, sleeping in my bed, making long slow love to me. I was finally reaping the rewards for my patience in waiting on him.

THE END

Here is a sample from another story you may enjoy:

I'll Never Find Another You

FRESHMAN AWAKENING

GAY ROMANCE

Dick Parker

It was the first day of classes on my first day in college. I was pretty nervous. I came from a small town and a small high school and now here I was in on a campus with more students than the number of people who lived in my town.

I saw him sit down three rows in front of me and to the side in the big lecture hall. Actually the lecture hall was an auditorium in the oldest building on campus. It was used for large lectures and this was one of those lectures, World History. I'm not sure why he stood out from the hundred or so other kids in the class but he caught my eye immediately.

At first I thought maybe I'd seen him someplace recently like at orientation or something but that didn't seem right.

I looked at him from the back and side and he looked interesting. I'd noticed him just as he sat down and he looked like he was about 5-foot eight or so. I didn't get a very good look but what I did see from the side he looked really handsome. His hair was medium length, and cut in that messy style that looked like he'd just gotten up from bed. It was light brown and he'd had blond highlights put in it and it was really hot looking. He turned a little and I was right, he was a good-looking guy. Then I caught myself.

I turned away and shook my head.

"What the hell am I doing looking at that guy?" I thought. "I'm not gay. I have no interest in some random guy."

The professor started lecturing from the stage and I began taking notes. Every now and then I'd catch myself sneaking a peak at the kid who I'd noticed. Each time I told myself to forget him, I had no interest in him.

My mind wasn't on the lecture. Maybe I was just excited about my new life in college and something made that guy stand out to me. It had to be something like that. I had no interest in guys. I never had.

The lecture was finally over and everyone started getting up to leave. The kid got up and stretched and his tee shirt rode up on his belly revealing about three inches of skin. The belly I could see looked real nice, with a light treasure trail disappearing into the top of his shorts and I found my cock feeling like it was about to bone up.

"Holy shit," I thought to myself, "You're getting a boner in class. Stop it!"

I turned and went out of the row of seats the opposite direction of the kid and walked to the exit. As I pushed on the door to open it another hand touched it at the same time and I turned and it was him.

"Sorry," he said, "go ahead."

He stepped back and I walked through. He followed me out of the room.

"Kind'a boring," he said.

"Huh?"

"The lecture, the Dark Ages, it was a little boring."

"Um yeah, it was."

I turned and almost ran down the hall to the outside door of the building. I pushed through and walked out onto the campus. My heart was beating like I'd just run a marathon.

"What the hell is wrong with me?" I asked myself.

I stood there in the sunlight trying to get my bearings and the kid walked past.

"See ya tomorrow," he said.

"Yeah," I said.

Damn, what the hell was going on? I wasn't gay. I'd had girlfriends in high school.

I watched the kid walk away and felt my cock tingling. He was wearing tan cargo shorts and sandals. He had gorgeous legs and feet and was built really well. After seeing him up close my thought that he was kind of cute was justified. Up close he was a beauty. He had gorgeous blue eyes and a perfect nose, perfect lips and beautiful white teeth. He was a really cute guy.

But what the hell was I doing thinking about another boy who was cute? What the fuck?

I went to my next three classes, had lunch and then went back to my dorm room. My roommate was in class so I kicked off my shoes and took off my shirt and lay on my bed holding a book in my hands but not reading.

All I could think about was that kid from World History. His face was in my mind and the more I thought about him the harder my cock got. Then my mind flashed on his bare stomach and the little light brown treasure trail that disappeared on his shorts. I wondered what his dick looked like.

I closed my eyes and rubbed my hand over my cock. I took hold of it through my shorts and began rubbing it. Damn I was horny.

Finally I gave in and unzipped my shorts and pulled them and my boxers down and took my cock in my hand. I closed my eyes and began jacking off and I was picturing that kid in my mind, naked and lying next to me. It didn't take long and I got the feeling. I reached up and grabbed a handful of Kleenex from my dresser and shot a big gob of cum into them.

I was lying there basking in the afterglow of sex when I heard my roommate say something to someone in the hall. I quickly reached down and pulled up my shorts and boxers just as he came into the room.

He looked at me and grinned.

"Were you jacking off?"

"Um no, I was…"

He grinned. "Hey, it's nothing to me. I do it every day. I bet every guy in this dorm does it daily or more."

I grinned at him.

"Okay, you caught me."

"Just don't get cum on my stuff," he said laughing.

"Okay I promise."

I buttoned my shorts and threw my wad of Kleenex in the wastebasket. My roommate was a good guy and I was lucky to have a guy I got along with. His name was David and he was from Minnesota and had a steady girlfriend who also went to this school so he was out of the room a lot. We really didn't have a lot in common, him being from a big city and me being from a small rural town.

I'd been a hunter and fisherman all my life and he had gone fishing once when he was a little kid. I'd had a couple of girlfriends in high school and he'd met his girlfriend when they were sophomores and they were still going together. He was a nice guy.

I broke open a book and started studying and so did David. The time passed quickly and I even managed to keep the kid from World History out of my mind.

"Are you going to eat dinner?" David asked.

I looked up and saw it was nearly 6 o'clock.

"Holy shit, no wonder I'm so hungry," I said.

We closed up our books and walked across the campus two blocks to the Food Center. There were several dorms in the three-block section of campus and the Food Center served meals to all of the students living in the dorms. We got in line and got our food and walked out into the dining room. There were probably two hundred kids eating at the time.

We saw a couple of guys from our floor of the dorm and joined them at their table. The talk was of the upcoming football game on Saturday and one of the guys was commenting on our quarterback when I saw the kid walk into the room. He was with a couple of guys and they were talking as they walked toward a table behind the one I was at.

He'd changed after class and was wearing gym shorts and a red tank top. I could plainly see his cock swinging under the shorts. He had on flip-flops on his feet.

Just as they sat down the kid looked up and noticed me. He grinned and waved. I smiled back and waved back at him.

"Who's that?" David asked.

"I don't know his name. He's in my history class."

And for the rest of the time I was in the dining room, my mind was on him. I didn't hear much of what was being said at my table but snuck glances at him as he ate and talked with his friends. They were laughing about something. I found myself smiling as I watched him. Damn he was pretty.

"Oh my God," I thought. "Did I just think that kid was pretty? What the hell is going on with me?"

"Mike. Mike. Hey earth to Mike."

I looked at David.

"What?"

"Where were you?"

"I was… I was thinking about something I guess."

"You got a chick on your mind?"

"Yeah something like that." I said.

Fuck me!

If you enjoyed this sample then look for **Freshman Awakening**.

From the Author

If you enjoyed any of my books then please share the love and click like on my books in Amazon.

If you write me a review and send me an email I will send you a free book, or many.
(Just know that these emails are filtered by my publisher.)

Good news is always welcome.

One Last Thing, For Kindle Readers...

When you turn the page, Kindle will give you the opportunity to rate this book and share your thoughts on Facebook and Twitter. If you enjoyed my writings, would you please take a few seconds to let your friends know about it? Because... when they enjoy they will be grateful to you and so will I.

Thank You!

Lamort DeLioncourt
lamort_delioncourt@awesomeauthors.org